Accidental

Ashes

That time I found out I was a demon,
and all my friends were vampires and
werewolves

Sara C. Roethle

Vulture's Eye Publications
Sierra Vista, AZ

Accidental Ashes: that time I found out I was a demon
and all my friends were vampires and werewolves.
The second book in the Xoe Meyers Fantasy/Horror
Series
Copyright ©2011 by Sara C. Roethle

Young Adult Fantasy/Horror
ISBN 978-0-615-48124-1

Published by Vulture's Eye Publications

Cover image and design by Nathaniel Goldstock

Vulture's Eye Publications
www.vultureseyepublications.com

Manufactured in the United States of America

Dedication

To my dad, for putting up with all of my random hippy gallivanting ways.

Acknowledgements

Special thanks: To my Sarah muffincakes, for her editing and enthusiasm. To Susan D. Kalior, who is always helping me out in these matters. To Nate, for meeting all of my cover design demands. To my dad, for helping me with everything else. And to all of my family and friends, who have been unfalteringly supportive of me.

Chapter One

I was sitting on the green loveseat in my living room. Jason was beside me with his arm around my shoulders. I curled my legs up against his lap, content. I glanced over at the larger blue couch where Lucy, Allison, and Max sat.

In the few months since we'd met him, Max had managed to get us all addicted to watching soccer, which we were all doing now.

Suddenly, Max leapt out of his seat, spilling popcorn on the carpet. "Go! Go!" he shouted.

It was World Cup time, and the game was USA against Mexico. One of the USA players had the ball and was running ahead of all of the opposing team towards their goal. Now, I hadn't quite gotten a grasp on the rules yet, but I could tell this was a good thing. The rest of us jumped out of our seats and joined Max in cheering the player on. One of the Mexico Players was gaining on him.

"Ruuuun!" Max shouted while clamping his fingers onto his shaggy, sandy colored hair as if in pain. To say that Max was enthusiastic about soccer was an understatement. When you're around someone that devout, you can't help but get caught up in the excitement.

I watched the TV screen, unblinking as the Mexico player surpassed the USA player. Suddenly they collided and both went down. One of the refs came running up to the fallen players, blowing his whistle and yelling something at the USA player. The USA player got to his feet and started yelling back. Uh-oh. The ref whipped out a red card and threw the USA player off the field.

"What!" Max shouted, throwing his hands in the air. "That ref is delusional . . ." Max began a tirade, his pale green eyes squinted in anger.

I got caught up in the moment and started yelling at the TV along with Max, feeling a sudden surge of anger at what Max deemed an unfair call.

Then the TV exploded. Crap. Did I mention that I'm a half-demon?

The past few months had been eventful, to say the least. A stranger named Dan had come to town. He happened to be a werewolf. Because of him, my best friend Lucy is a werewolf now too. With the help of Max (also a werewolf), and Jason (vampire), we had managed to rid ourselves of Dan. I won't go into the grisly details on *how* we rid ourselves of him. Let's just say that the event made me question my moral fiber more than a little.

Amid all of this chaos, I found out that my dad, whom I've never met, is a demon, making me a half-demon. Demons aren't bad or anything. Well, not *all* demons are bad. At least, that's what Jason tells me. I have an inkling suspicion that he only says that to make me feel better. Yet, seeing as I'm the only demon I know, I'll just have to take his word for it.

At the explosion my friends all went completely silent, then turned in slow-motion to regard me as one. I looked back to the TV. The screen had completely shattered, and the frame was a charred mess. Heaps of black smoke poured out of its smoldering innards to fill my living room with an acrid stench.

I stood under the pressure of their gazes only long enough to turn on my heel and run across my living room. I went right out my front door, slamming it behind me. I heard the door open and shut again as I ran into the tall pine trees that border my house. The scent of pine and crisp air hit me, instantly clearing my senses. I wasn't sure I wanted them cleared at the moment.

This had been happening to me a lot lately, the blowing up of random appliances thing. When my powers as a half-demon first manifested, I had burned my friend Brian just by touching him. Since then, I'd graduated to blowing things up or just lighting them on fire. My powers were related to my temper, and that temper was mighty hard to control these days. Even the most insignificant things could make me mad enough to do some real damage. I couldn't control it, and the threat of what could happen weighed on me constantly.

I stood trembling in the dark, silent trees, my arms wrapped tightly around me. I would not cry. I would not cry about the stupid TV. The moisture that I felt slipping down my face was simply a raindrop. Yeah, a raindrop, that's it. I heard footsteps behind me, then felt arms gently wrap around me from behind.

I leaned back against Jason's chest and tried to take comfort in his presence. I unclenched my arms and rubbed my hands across the blue flannel shirt that encased his arms. I felt a slight bit of tension leave my body, but not nearly enough.

"You do not need to be so upset about it," he murmured. "We all understand." Jason talks kinda funny, probably due to the fact that he was born in 1883. You would think he'd have picked up more on modern speech, given the fact that he'd been around to see it evolve, but he'd spent most of his life as a vampire alone, up until now at least.

"I know you're all used to it by now," I said between sniffles. "I just hate not being able to control it. What if it's one of you next time?"

Jason squeezed me a little tighter, keeping me warm despite the fact that I was only wearing a gray cotton t-shirt and jeans in Oregon, in December. He brushed his lips against my cheek. "We must simply be sure that we do not make you mad," he said, trying to lighten the mood, "though it is a somewhat difficult task these days."

I struggled out of his arms and turned to point a finger in his smiling face. "This is no time to crack jokes."

He put his arms up in mock surrender. "Oh no! Do not burn me!"

I pouted as I returned my hand to my side. "I could you know. I could hurt you, or Lucy, or Al, or Max."

Jason lowered his hands and took on a more serious tone. "You will not harm us. You have more control than you think. Otherwise you would have blown me up a thousand times over."

I crossed my arms and pretended to consider what he said. I nodded. "True, very true."

Jason smiled. "Come now my little demon, back inside."

I stomped my sneaker-clad foot on the hard, damp soil. "Half-demon," I corrected sharply.

"Of course," he conceded. Then before I could react, he picked me up and threw me across his shoulder to carry me back inside.

I fake struggled, shouting, "I'll burn you! Don't tempt me!"

He paused and hoisted me up, getting a more secure hold on me. "I am well and truly terrified," he replied. Jason easily held onto me with one hand while he opened the front door and walked us inside.

By the time Jason managed to plop me back down on the couch, Lucy had swept up all of the TV bits and was emptying the dustpan in the kitchen. Jason left me to help Max lift what remained of the TV frame to take it outside, where it would await a ride to the dump. Poor TV. I didn't know how I was going to explain this one to my mom. I mean, appliances only set fire so often. The toaster and the washing machine had each already met their untimely demise.

Jason returned to sit beside me on the couch, wrapping his arm around my shoulders again. Allison came to stand in front of me while shrugging on her fake-fur lined coat. She pushed her long honey blonde hair behind her ears, then leaned down and kissed me on the cheek. "We're taking off Xoe. Call me tomorrow."

I gave her a feeble wave goodbye. Lucy leaned over the back of the couch to give me a hug, enfolding me in her petite arms and long, pin-straight black hair. As soon as Lucy backed away, Max gave my shoulder a comforting squeeze, and soon I was alone with Jason. For a little while anyway; my mom would be home from doing her Christmas shopping soon.

I snuggled up against Jason's broad, muscled chest (not over-muscled mind you. I like my men lean). His hand lifted to stroke my pale blond hair. It had grown long enough to brush past my shoulders. I was overdue for a cut.

I turned my head so I could look into Jason's deep blue eyes, and I do mean deep blue, like the color of the sky just before it turns to black. I'd never seen eyes that could be that dark and still manage to look blue until I met him. "Sorry I'm so messed up right now," I said quietly. "I just can't seem to get used to all of this demon stuff."

Jason smiled down at me warmly. "It is a lot to take in. You are doing well, given the circumstances."

I looked back down at my lap, feeling like a failure despite his encouragement.

Jason continued to watch me, being far too observant for his own good. "What is wrong Xoe? I can tell you have something to say."

I debated for a few seconds on whether or not I wanted to tell him. I sighed. Here goes nothing. "The dreams started again."

Several months ago, before my life went to hell-in-a-hand-basket, I had started having these dreams, and I always awoke with a fever. I dreamed of fire, then I found out that I was part demon. A wolf was in one of my dreams, and my best friend got turned into a werewolf.

Once things had calmed down, I'd finally confided in Jason about the dreams. The only other people who had known were my mom and Lucy. Jason had instantly come to the conclusion that I had a minor gift at premonition, and it had come out in my dreams.

Jason's arms tightened around me slightly. "Tell me."

"Well," I began. "The fire's back, for starters, but this time none of my friends or family are there." I had seen my mom and my friends consumed by the flames in my previous dreams. "At first, I think that I'm alone, then I feel a presence at my side. I blink, and when I open my eyes, there is a man silhouetted against the flames. I can't see him, but I somehow know him. Then, he turns away from me and jumps into the fire."

Jason was silent for a moment. He snuggled a little closer to me, if that was even possible. "Do you have any idea what it means?" he asked.

I shook my head morosely. "Not a clue, but I don't like it."

"Nor do I," he replied quietly. "Have you told anyone else?"

I shook my head. "Nope. There's no sense in worrying the others. It could be nothing."

He gave me a very knowing smile. "Or it could very well be something. It cannot hurt to have everyone on their guard."

"But on guard for what? We don't even know who the man in the dream is."

"All the more reason to be prepared for anything," he countered.

I pursed my full lips into a pout. "So, in other words, you're not just gonna let me ignore it in the hopes that it goes away?"

"Like you did with me?" he joked.

I shoved away from him playfully. "I did *not*."

"Yes, uh-huh," he replied. "You utterly refused to admit your feelings for me until after we almost died."

I raised my eyebrows coyly. "Who says I have feelings for you?"

He grabbed me and pulled me close again. "I'm a vampire," he answered dramatically. "We can sense these things."

Our banter was interrupted by the sound of a key in the door. A few seconds later, my mom walked in, hands full of shopping bags. She threw her bags on the floor and stripped off her khaki, knee-length trench to reveal dark-wash jeans and a dark brown, cable-knit sweater. Her newly shoulder length, dark brown wavy hair blended into the sweater so that you couldn't tell where one stopped and the other began. She walked towards us and threw her coat across the back of the loveseat. "Hey you two, what are you . . . where's the TV?"

I smiled nervously.

"Not again?" my mom sighed loudly in her rich, throaty voice. I like to lie to myself and pretend that my voice sounds like her's, but in reality mine's an octave or so higher. Though our voices are the least of our differences. My pale skinned, green eyed genetics were obviously not passed on from my mom's side. Our looks are on opposite sides of the color spectrum.

I nodded, trying to hold my nervous smile in place. "I think, maybe, we have like, an electrical problem or something?"

My mom put her hands on her hips. "An electrical problem that causes household appliances to spontaneously combust?"

Jason and I both shrugged.

My mom stared at us skeptically, then turned to re-gather her shopping bags. I couldn't imagine what she actually thought about the exploding appliances. She had played it pretty cool so far, but her observant patience could only last so long.

My mom stopped to regard us again before she went up the stairs to her bedroom. "I'll call the electrician tomorrow." Then, when she reached the top she shouted. "And it's 9:00!"

9:00 was my "boy curfew," 11:00 on weekends. After that, Jason either had to go home, or if we were out, I had to come home. Jason reached up and touched my face, gently guiding me towards him. He leaned forward and met my lips for a chaste kiss. His lips were warm and soft against mine. I lifted my arms to wrap behind his neck, twining my fingers in his tousled dark brown hair. The kiss turned a little less chaste. Before I knew it, I had scooted onto Jason's lap. His arms circled my waist and pulled me against him. I sank into his warmth, feeling my troubles melt away. This was a relatively new feeling for me, feeling absolutely safe in someone's arms. My dad had never been around, and as hard as my mom tried, she just didn't really fit into the big, strong protector role. Up until now, I'd always felt that I simply had to protect myself. It wasn't a bad feeling, but it could be lonely. In other words, it wasn't about needing to be protected, I just enjoyed finally having the option. Our little session went on for a while longer, until I reluctantly pulled back.

I met his dark blue eyes again and almost dove back in for more. Sadly, I managed to restrain myself. "See you tomorrow?"

He gave me one more gentle kiss. "You could not keep me away."

He was up and out the door in 5 seconds flat. It still unnerved me how quickly he moved. It was even more unnerving when Lucy did it, though she wasn't as fast as Jason. I wasn't very fast at all, and not for lack of trying. Hanging out with werewolves and a vampire all of the time had brought me to the conclusion that I was the worst half-demon ever. I just couldn't compete.

During my reverie I checked to make sure that Jason had locked the front door behind him, which he had, as always, then I journeyed upstairs to my bedroom. I got ready for bed in the adjoining purple themed bathroom, then changed into green flannel pj pants and an oversized David Bowie t-shirt. I sat down on my dark green comforter and hugged a yellow cased pillow to my chest. I was so not ready for bed.

I looked over at my computer desk with its backdrop of old-school horror movie posters, and contemplated surfing the web for a while. Finally, I settled on snuggling up in bed and reading my copy of Stephen King's *Desperation* that Jason had recently purchased for me.

When I finally shut off the lights, I gave a weak prayer that I wouldn't dream. Fat chance.

Chapter Two

Fire was all around me. I'd become rather used to fire, in the dream-world as well as in the real one. I sat cross-legged on a cold stone floor and watched the shadows of the flames dance in the darkness around me. I wasn't scared, I was more . . . peaceful.

I looked to my side to see the man from my previous dream was sitting beside me in the same cross-legged position. I couldn't see his face, but once again felt like I somehow knew him. He held up one hand and snapped his fingers. A small flame appeared in-between his thumb and index finger, as if he'd lit a lighter, only there wasn't any lighter. Flames reflected off his teeth as his mouth curled into a smile, though the rest of his face remained hidden in shadow.

I slowly lifted my hand and mimicked his actions, producing a small flame of my own. I stared at my hand and smiled, pleased with what I had accomplished, though normally my powers didn't please me at all. This seemed to be one I actually had some control over.

When I turned back to smile at the man, he was gone, and the fire was gone from my surroundings. The smile slipped from my face as I realized I'd been left alone in the cool, stone darkness.

I woke at 8:10am. It was a Tuesday, but it was also winter break, so no school. Hallelujah. I cringed upon remembering that my wish for a dreamless night had not been granted. My pajamas were soaked with sweat from the inevitable fever.

I dragged myself out of bed and padded barefoot downstairs for breakfast. My mom had already left for work, and had left me a half-pot of coffee, bless her soul. The cold tiles of my cheerful kitchen were a shock in my partially-awake state. I grabbed a blue ceramic mug from one of the maple colored cabinets and filled it to the top, foregoing cream. I stayed standing in my sunny yellow kitchen for a few minutes enjoying my coffee and looking out the kitchen window to the lush vegetation. This had become my Winter Break morning ritual.

As I watched, Brian came trotting out of the front door of his house, wearing light gray sweats with his short curly brown hair still frizzy from sleep. He paused and glanced in the direction of my house. I gasped and sidestepped out of view of the window, sloshing scalding coffee on my hand. I stood silently cursing, waiting for Brian to move on.

Brian had been one of my best friends, that is, until I'd accidentally burned him with my newfound demon powers. I had passed out shortly after. While I was unconscious, Lucy and Allison had filled Brian in on everything: demons, werewolves, and the whole kit and caboodle. Brian had not taken it well. He hadn't spoken to me since.

A knot formed in my throat at the memory. I took a deep steadying breath, telling myself that I was done crying over the ordeal. I stole a quick glance out the window to see Brian trotting down the road on his morning run. I grabbed a paper towel to blot the cooling coffee off my hand and the floor. As I dried off my hand, I realized that the coffee hadn't left a burn. In fact, my hand wasn't even the slightest bit red. Another Demon power? I guess it would make sense. I could burn other people without getting burnt myself. Maybe I couldn't get burned period. Had I actually gained a power that didn't have any drawbacks? I smiled and headed upstairs to take a shower with a little extra spring in my step. Maybe I'd make my water extra hot, just because I could.

My bathroom hadn't changed much in the last year: purple rug and towels, marble-tiled shower, pedestal sink beneath a large circular mirror. I turned on the shower and waited for it to heat up, then stripped off my pajamas and stepped in. The hot water eased tension in my shoulders that I hadn't even realized was there. I started washing my hair with my new lemongrass scented shampoo, while going over a mental checklist of the things I needed to do today.

I needed to go Christmas shopping. I had managed to save up eighty dollars of my allowance money for that purpose, since I don't have a job. Hopefully Jason wouldn't mind giving me a ride for said Christmas shopping, since I don't have a car. I had also promised my mom that I would put together a bookshelf she had gotten at IKEA. My mom is horrible at directions, so such tasks usually fall to me. After all that was done, I was supposed to go to Lucy's house to bake cookies with her family. We did it every year.

Once squeaky clean, I stepped out of the shower and wrapped my fluffy purple towel around me. I used a blow-dryer on my hair, which was an addition to my routine that I had grudgingly accepted after much insistence from Allison. And no, I did not do it to impress Jason. I wanted to look good for me, damn it.

I got dressed in a burgundy sweater and faded jeans, then pulled on my faded gray sneakers. I got back downstairs just in time to hear a knock at my front door. I trotted up and unlocked to door to find Jason waiting outside, dressed in a charcoal fleece sweatshirt (Oregonians are big on fleece) and jeans. He held a stack of envelopes and a few catalogues in his hand. "Got your mail," he said, handing the pile to me.

I turned to go back into my living room with the mail gripped against my chest, leaving the door open for Jason to follow me in. I walked into the dining room, spilling the mail onto my rectangular, pale wood dining table. I started shuffling through the pile, looking for anything that might be addressed to me as Jason came into the room behind me. He pulled out a chair done in the same pale wood as the table with a bright yellow seat cushion that matched the placemats. He sat quietly watching me, as he often does. It used to make me uncomfortable, but I've gotten used to it.

I lifted a white business envelope that was addressed to Alexondra Meyers from the pile. I cringed at my un-shortened name as I examined the envelope skeptically (I don't usually get any mail). There was no return address. I glanced up at Jason and shrugged, then started

16

carefully tearing it open. I pulled out a folded white piece of computer paper that felt like it had a thick stack of paper inside. I unfolded it and a stack of one hundred dollar bills went tumbling to the table, held together by a thin strip of paper.

Shocked, I grabbed the money and held it up to Jason. He cocked his head. "Is there a note?"

As a matter of fact, there was. There was another piece of computer paper folded up inside the first one to accompany the bills. I slowly unfolded it, my fingertips feeling numb with shock.

"To Miss Alexondra Meyers,
Enclosed is your payment for aiding in the situation with our rogue wolf a few months back. Your vampire told us of your request to forgo monetary compensation, yet I feel I must go against your confusing wishes. I do not enjoy owing favors, and like it or not, without payment, that is exactly what I would owe you. I hope to work with you and your strange lot of friends in the future.
Sincerely,
Abel"

My jaw dropped. "It's from Abel," I stuttered.

Jason's midnight blue eyes widened in surprise. "I told him that you did not desire payment."

I nodded. "He says he doesn't want to owe me a favor."

Jason smiled wistfully at that. "Wolves can be strange with such things."

Some explanation. Abel was the alpha of the pack that Dan had run away from. Jason had originally been hired to track Dan until he entered an area with a local wolf pack, so that they could kill Dan because he had killed a human, breaking an unbending werewolf law. After things had gone bad, and Dan was reduced to a smoldering pile of ash, Abel and his wolves had come to clean up the mess.

I picked up the bills from where I had placed them on the counter. I started counting, placing each bill back on the table as I went. As the pile on the table grew larger, so did my utter disbelief. I placed the last bill on the pile and stood staring at it, unable to breathe, let alone speak.

"How much?" Jason questioned.

I didn't answer.

"Xoe? How much?"

I snapped out of my fog. "T-ten thousand dollars."

Jason simply nodded. "That is around what I would expect."

I peered at Jason, stunned. "Who on earth sends ten thousand dollars cash in the mail?"

Jason answered matter-of-factly. "Bounty hunters deal only in cash. I assume he would have delivered it in person if he could. He is a very busy man."

I collapsed into one of the dining room chairs. "What am I supposed to do with it?"

Jason cocked his head again, not understanding my question.

I clarified, "What am I supposed to do with ten thousand dollars cash? I can't very well open a bank account for it. I'm only sixteen. I can't open a bank account by myself period."

Jason nodded, taking in my dilemma. "If you would like, I will deposit whatever portion of it you desire into the savings portion of my account. I will order you a card so that you can withdraw it as you choose."

I nodded. "Well, at least I'll be able to do all of my Christmas shopping now."

Jason smiled. "Have you eaten breakfast? We can stop somewhere after we go to the bank if you would like."

I nodded and stood. Jason vacated his seat and waited for me to gather up my ridiculous amount of money before we headed for the front door. A thought dawned on me as we were sliding into Jason's fancy charcoal grey car. "If I got ten thousand just for doing the final deed, how much did you get?"

Jason smiled and put the car in drive. "Bounty hunting is a very lucrative business."

Chapter Three

When we got to the bank, I waited in the car, while Jason went inside to deposit my money. I'd kept one thousand of it out, figuring I'd spend it on Christmas presents. Plus I'd heard somewhere that if you deposit ten thousand dollars or more in a bank account the bank had to declare it to the IRS. That was as much as I knew about that subject, and Jason probably knew more than I did, but better safe than sorry. I think more than anything I was trying to avoid thinking about how guilty I felt about the money; it seemed all too much like blood-money. Dan totally had it coming, but I still felt like an assassin. Maybe buying big presents for my loved ones would take some of the weight off my conscience. Maybe.

Jason walked back out of the bank towards the car. A ray of sunshine peeked through the cloudy sky to reflect off his sunglasses. And no, my vampire doesn't sparkle. Jason slid back into the driver's seat and put his seatbelt on. "Your card should arrive in the mail within a few days, and you can set your pin number by phone. If you want any of your money before that, just let me know."

I smiled. "Can do. Where do you want to get breakfast?"

"IHOP?" he asked grinning.

Jason had developed a major penchant for IHOP. Until he met me, he had never even eaten there. And yes, I know what you're thinking. But isn't he a vampire? Yes, he is, but despite the legends, he eats people food, is awake during the day, and is rather fond of garlic.

I sighed loudly in mock exasperation. "Oooookay."

Jason put his hand on my leg with a grin and whipped out of the parking spot, driving like a maniac all the way to IHOP. Once we arrived, we were seated almost right away. After we slid into a corner booth by a window, we both ordered coffee and blintzes.

"So," I began while the waiter filled our cups. "How much did Abel give you?"

Jason looked down. I'd say he was embarrassed if I didn't know any better. "Five thousand," he answered.

I started to laugh, but held it in . . . mostly. "Why on earth did you get less than me?" I asked.

He grimaced. "Abel wasn't terribly pleased with the job I did."

My grin widened. "Really?"

Jason sighed loudly, seeing that I wasn't going to let it go. "My job was to keep an eye on Dan, and make sure he didn't cause any mischief, until such a time when a pack could take him into custody."

I cringed at his mention of Dan's "mischief." Yeah, mischief was one thing to call it. Some other useful words might have been havoc, destruction, mayhem . . . get the idea?

I said thanks as the waiter set our blintzes on the table, strawberry for me, blueberry for Jason, then turned back to our conversation. "So, can you handle being with a girl who makes more money than you?" I mocked.

He smiled wickedly. "Of course I can, as long as you realize one thing."

"And what's that?" I prompted.

He smugly took a bite of his blintz and swallowed with a satisfied grin. "That the breadwinner in the relationship has to pay for breakfast."

I pouted. "You know what?"

"What?" he asked before shoving more blintz into his mouth.

"Wearing the pants totally sucks."

He patted my hand in sympathy. "You'll get used to it."

I frowned. "Doubtful, very doubtful."

After a few minutes of eating in silence, I knew it was time for me to convince Jason of our next stop. "So…" I began with a flirtatious smile on my lips.

Jason ducked his head and smiled, knowing all to well what the smile meant. "Where are we going next?" he asked, feigning frustration.

"I gotta do my Christmas shopping," I stated sweetly.

"Can I just drop you off?" he asked hopefully.

I gasped and held my hands to my chest. "You would abandon little ol' me to fend for myself?"

He took his last swig of coffee then thumped the empty mug onto the table and smiled at me. "Not in a million years."

I laughed as we got up to leave, pleased that I'd gotten my way. And he payed for the food, so apparently the money thing hadn't hurt his pride *too* bad.

The shortest way to the mall passes right by Shelby's cemetery. Though the cemetery gives me the major creeps, pride would not allow me to suggest a different route. The cemetery has always creeped me out, but my phobia had become even worse since the Dan incident. The entire reason Dan had even decided to pass through Shelby was its large, old cemetery. I had always passed off the feeling I got in cemeteries as superstition, but Dan had informed me otherwise.

Cemeteries are full of magic; the older and larger the cemetery, the better. On the rare occasions I'd had to visit the cemetery, I'd felt like the spirits of the dead were pushing down on me, making the air thick in a very ominous sort of way. Apparently it was all of the loose, unused magic that made me feel like I was suffocating. Dan had used that magic to call demons.

I closed my eyes and took a deep breath as we drove by the cemetery. I felt Jason's hand give my leg a light squeeze. He must have sensed my discomfort. "Are you well?" he asked.

I nodded my head, but kept my eyes closed.

Jason let the subject drop. Smart man.

I opened my eyes when I was sure that we were past all the graves. It only took a minute more for us to reach Shelby's small mall. Jason turned into the parking lot and parked near one of the larger department stores. I waited in the car while he walked around to get my door for me. Yeah, I know, a little outdated, and I would have much rather just opened the door myself, but it made Jason happy to do it, so I waited in the car like a proper young lady. Who says I can't compromise?

I was slightly taken aback by the crowds of people and the blaring fluorescent lighting as we entered the mall. Nondescript Christmas music hummed in the background of the din of shopper's voices. It was almost as bad as the cemetery . . . almost.

Jason looked down at me. "Would you like to shop alone, or shall I stay with you?"

"Alone. I plan on getting *all* of my gift shopping done today, and that includes a gift for you." I gave Jason's hand a final squeeze as I prepared to brave the crowds on my own. As our hands parted he walked backwards for a moment, smiling at me, before turning around to walk in the direction of the food court. I gave myself a shake when I realized that I was ogling him as he walked away. C'mon Xoe, focus on the task at hand.

After the first few stores, I was nearly done with my shopping, which was a great relief. I'd purchased a new purse for Allison (Allison wasn't big on my fashion sense, but I figured the big price on the tag would make up for it), an expensive, high-tech toothbrush for Lucy (it might seem like a lame gift, but Lucy was strangely obsessive about oral hygiene, and I knew she'd like it), and I splurged on a necklace for my mom that had a delicate bird pendant.

I headed over to the sports store to get something soccer related for Max. As soon as I entered the colorful store, I noticed a Dallas Cowboys football jersey hanging on the wall, and felt a small twinge of sadness. They were Brian's favorite team, and this would be the first year that Brian and I wouldn't be exchanging Christmas gifts. That sadness quickly turned to anger. It wasn't my damn fault that we wouldn't be exchanging gifts. *He* was the one that stopped talking to *me*.

I quickly turned my anger into quiet determination (didn't want to blow anything up). An idea came to me. Brian might be able to keep me from talking to him, but I'd be damned if he'd keep me from buying him a Christmas present. I'd just leave it by his door sometime when he wasn't home. I could be a good friend and spite him all at the same time.

With my spirits somewhat restored, I went to the counter to get a sales guy to get the jersey down for me. The sales guy was short and blond, *so* not my type, but he seemed to think otherwise. He wasted an overly friendly smile on me as he tried to maintain eye contact with me. I am not a casual flirter by any means. Not only do I suck at it, it makes me horribly uncomfortable.

I pointed to the jersey I wanted and grunted something unintelligible about not being able to reach it.

Taking my discomfort for nervousness, the sales guy smiled even wider. "I wouldn't expect you to be able to reach it. It's only a good ten feet out of your reach."

He'd meant the comment to be cute, but I scowled at him in return. An awkward silence ensued until he finally went to get my jersey. While he was busy I picked out a Manchester United jersey for Max. The sales guy returned, obviously not trying to flirt anymore. He silently rung me up and handed me my purchases. If

I were Allison, I would have flirted back and procured a discount. But I wasn't Allison, and I didn't need no stinkin' discounts.

I took my bag and turned on my heel to leave. I checked my receipt before putting it in the bag and noticed that blondie had written his phone number on it. I had to give him points for persistence.

I turned my thoughts to more pressing matters. The only person left for me to buy for was Jason, and I had no idea what to get him. I left the sports store and started walking down the mall hallway, mind preoccupied with trying to come up with something Jason would like.

As my mind was shuffling through gift options, someone walked up behind me and grabbed my wrist. I turned, thinking it was Jason, and looked into bright green eyes the exact color of my own. I dropped my shopping bags in surprise, causing a group of mall patrons to split up and give me a wide berth. I looked up from my fallen bags to take in the rest of the stranger that still had a hold of my wrist. He was tall, probably about 6'3", and had straight blond hair, artfully swept back off of his face to almost reach his shoulders. He was dressed in a pale green, expensive looking sweater that looked bland in comparison to his eyes along with charcoal gray slacks.

My mouth went dry, he looked . . . like me. From his narrow nose, to his somewhat full lips that looked almost out of place on his angular face, he was the male version of me.

He smiled, still holding my wrist. "It's very good to see you Alexondra."

I didn't return the smile. "Unfortunately I can't say the same."

His smile didn't falter, not one single inch. "Now, is that any way to speak to your father?"

My heart raced. He'd confirmed what I had already figured out. I began to shake with the effort to contain the sudden anger that washed over me. I spoke slowly through gritted teeth, "Let . . go . . of . . me."

He didn't. I began to tremble almost violently. All of the pain and anger I had blocked out over the years came flooding back. He'd abandoned me. My mom had never even told me his name.

As if reading my mind, he said, "I'm going to assume that you would rather not call me dad, so you may call me Alexondre.'

Well, now I knew where I got my name, though I couldn't imagine why my mom would want to name me after someone that had abandoned her too. I took a deep breath. "Why are you here?"

"You're almost seventeen. I'm here to help you come into your powers . . . unless you already have?"

I smiled bitterly. "Yeah, you're a little late on that one."

He furrowed his brow as if he actually felt sorry about being late. "How late am I?" he asked.

I rolled my eyes in irritation. "Seventeen years."

"I meant how late am I on the powers? Speaking of which, stop trying to burn me. It won't work."

My eyes widened in surprise. I knew I was angry enough for it, but I didn't realize that I was trying to burn him . . . not that I felt bad for trying.

"It's that bad?" he asked, referring to my lack of control.

"Well what did you expect?" I snapped. "I didn't even know I was different until a werewolf smelled me. I had to figure out what I could do by burning one of my friends!" I shouted.

A couple walking by with a small child between them veered farther away from me as they passed, sandwiching themselves closer to the child. The woman looked at me like I was crazy. Of course, I was shouting nonsense in the middle of a crowded mall, so maybe she was right.

Out of nowhere, Jason suddenly appeared beside me and grabbed Alexondre's wrist, since Alexondre was still gripping mine. Alexandre gave Jason such a look that I was surprised Jason didn't just turn into stone on the spot.

Alexondre's grip on my wrist was as strong as ever. He turned his gaze back to me. "Do you know this vampire?"

I raised my eyebrows and nodded in a 'well duh' gesture.

Alexondre slowly let go of my wrist as Jason slowly let go of his. They stood staring at each other, both of them trying to loom, though they were nearly the same height, so neither had much success.

Without looking at me, Alexondre spoke, "We need to talk Alexandra. You may have survived the beginnings of your powers on your own, but you'll need a teacher."

"Yes I do," I spoke crisply, "but it's not gonna be you."

I grabbed Jason's arm with one hand and gathered my bags with the other, then made a beeline for the door. Alexondre watched us go impassively, but didn't follow.

As soon as we were both buckled into Jason's car, he turned to me. "He is right."

"What?" I asked skeptically.

Jason avoided my gaze. "You need a teacher."

I kept my eyes looking steadily out the front window. "Not him."

"But . . . "

"Not him."

Jason let it drop. Like I said, smart man.

Chapter Four

We spent the ride home in silence. I didn't want Jason to think that I was mad at him, but my mind was spinning too much for me to even think about keeping up a conversation. I hadn't expected to ever hear from my dad, let alone run into him at the mall. But there he was, in the flesh . . . or whatever he was made of.

When we got home I stormed into my house, marching straight up to my bedroom. Jason walked in a few seconds behind me, to find me sitting on my bed, already sinking into a fugue. He silently approached and sat beside me, wrapping his arm around my lower back.

His comfort made my emotions fade from anger to hurt confusion. I looked down at my hands, not wanting to meet Jason's eyes. "She named me after him."

"His name is Alexondra?" Jason asked quizzically.

I shook my head and let out an abrupt laugh that was more of a sob. I grabbed Jason's hand where it was resting on the side of my waist and pulled it farther forward to encircle my stomach, and bring him closer to me. "Alexondre. His name's Alexondre, but it's close enough."

Jason kissed me lightly on the cheek, waiting for me to continue speaking. When I didn't, he said, "Please just consider it."

Sigh. Back to the subject of Alexondre being my teacher. I nodded slowly, knowing that he was right. "I'll try." Yeah, I'd try as hard as I tried in math class. Did I mention that I'm failing?

He took me at my word, or else he was simply letting the subject drop. "What time are you supposed to be at Lucy's?"

I looked at my *Jack Skellington* wall clock. His face was the face of the clock, and he had a little plastic body that swung back and forth in place of a pendulum. It was already close to 3:15. "Like fifteen minutes ago."

Jason gave me a final squeeze. "I will drive you."

We went back downstairs to gather all my bags from where I had thrown them on the floor on my way in. After taking everything back up to my room, Jason drove me the short distance to Lucy's.

Jason parked in the circular, gravel driveway in front of Lucy's two-story house. I gave him a quick kiss goodbye and hopped out of his car to walk to the front door. After knocking on the dark wood, I waited in the shade of the awning for someone to let me in. Lucy's mom opened the door a crack to see who was outside, then opened it the rest of the way when she saw that it was me.

Lucy's mom is even shorter than Lucy, about 4'11". I used to be terrified of her when I was younger. She is a very stoic woman, whose mouth is always set in a firm, unrelenting line. Her eyes, which are the same almond shape as Lucy's, regarded me with calculating interest, then turned and walked towards the kitchen, expecting me to follow.

"Nice to see you too," I mumbled to empty air as I stepped over the threshold. I waved goodbye to Jason before shutting the door behind me and taking off my shoes. I placed them on the small square of tiling in front of the door, then headed to the kitchen.

As soon as I walked into the pristine fluorescence, I was met by a screeching seven year-old. "Xoe!" Lucy's little sister Lizzie shouted as she hurled herself at me. I lifted her up underneath her armpits and spun her in a quick circle, making her long-sleeved yellow dress flare out. Lizzie looks like a miniature Lucy: long, dark, pin-straight hair, olive skin, and almond eyes, but instead of Lucy's small, cupid's-bow mouth, she has a wide mouth always formed into a smile to split her face in half. Since Allison and I are only children, we both love being around Lucy's sister.

Lucy smiled at me from her seat at the small oak table that stood in the kitchen near the entrance. She had on a white apron over her deep purple v-neck sweater and khaki slacks to protect them from the flour and cookie frosting. Lucy's mom stood silently over the kitchen counter, rolling out some cookie dough on wax paper beside the assorted Christmas cookie cutters she had already set out. Above the cookie cutters was an array of colored frostings and sprinkles for decorating the cookies after they were baked. Lucy's mom finished her rolling and walked out of the kitchen silently. A woman of few words, was Lucy's mom.

After we had cut and baked the cookies, Lucy set Lizzie to the task of decorating at the small table, so that she could pull me aside. We stood in the corner of the kitchen by the clean, magnet-free refrigerator. Lizzie hummed over her cookies with her back to us, completely absorbed in her task.

I looked down at Lucy questioningly.

She held my gaze firmly with her deep brown eyes. "I have news," she whispered.

I lifted my shoulders then let them down with a deep sigh. "So do I," I admitted with a matching whisper.

Lucy cocked her head curiously. "You first."

I shook my head silently and pointed a finger at Lucy, signaling for her to start.

"Lela's still in town."

"What?" I whispered incredulously. Lela had been one of Dan's flunkies. Upon meeting her, she had thrown Allison into a wall and then moved on to attacking me. I'd been forced to stop her with a fireplace poker to the side of her head. Lela wasn't all bad though. Once she had been separated from Dan, she was all too eager to join our side. She had wanted rid of Dan just as much as the rest of us. "How do you know?" I whispered.

Lucy rolled her eyes. "She showed up on my doorstep this morning."

"What are you two whispering about?" Lizzie chimed in loudly.

"Boys," I lied.

Lizzie made a disgusted sound. "You guys are gross."

Lucy gave me an angry look (Lucy's mom stood by the belief that her daughters didn't even know what boys were) and raised her eyebrows at me, waiting for me to apologize.

I shrugged, and nodded over to Lizzie, who had duteously gone back to her cookies. I brought us back to subject. "What did she want?"

Lucy still looked a little irritated, but answered, "She says she wants to talk to you, me, and Max. She refused to say anything else until she could talk to the three of us together."

"Why me?" I asked, confused.

"What do you mean 'why you?'"

"Well, I can understand her wanting to talk to you and Max, since you're both werewolves," I explained, "but why would she want to talk to me?"

Lucy considered for a moment. "I don't know, but I told her we would meet at your place at 7:00 tonight. I already called Max."

I managed to close my gaping jaw enough to complain, "Geez, thanks a lot for filling me in."

Lucy shook her head, brushing off my sarcasm. "What's your news?"

"Well," I began, "Lela's not the only one who's in town."

Lucy turned away from me as her mom strode into the kitchen to silently admire Lizzie's handiwork. When her mom left, Lucy turned back to me expectantly.

"Jason and I went to the mall today," I explained. "We ran into my dad."

Now it was Lucy's petite jaw that hung agape. "Your dad? Are you sure? How did you know it was him?"

I looked down, no longer able to meet Lucy's gaze. "It was him, no doubt about it. We had a rather unpleasant conversation."

Lucy shook her head with disbelief. "Let's go to your place," she glanced at Lizzie, "away from prying ears."

I nodded and walked over to where Lizzie was still happily decorating cookies with Lucy following shortly behind me. In the short time she'd had to work, Lizzie had managed to cover each and every cookie with globs of multi-colored frosting, and was now covering them with a thick coating of sprinkles. Lizzie smiled up at me, showcasing the fact that about half of the frosting had gone around her mouth. Lucy sighed and started cleaning up the mess.

After we finished, Lucy and I began the short walk to my house. Lucy didn't let the silence stand for long. "So what did your dad say?"

I watched my sneakers as we walked over the faded asphalt of our street. "He wants to teach me," I answered.

"Teach you what?" Lucy interrupted.

"About being a demon, and learning to control my powers."

"Oh," Lucy answered.

'Oh' was right. I still hadn't gotten any nearer to coming to terms with my feelings on the situation. I could play apathetic to things all I wanted, but in reality, I was furious with my dad. I didn't think I could stand to be around him long enough to ever forgive him for leaving my mom and me. Yet, though I hated to admit it, there was a deep down part of me that had always hoped he would come back.

I huddled against the cold breeze, wishing I'd worn a jacket over my burgundy sweater, and stared out into our green surroundings. Most of the trees in Shelby are evergreens, making fall and winter much more green than in other areas. I let the silence draw on until we reached my house. My mom's car was gone, so she was either working late, or out Christmas shopping.

Lucy and I went in through the front door and into my colorful living room. The deep green loveseat was occupied with rolls of Christmas-themed wrapping paper and ribbons that my mom had kept from last year, so Lucy sat down on the dark blue couch. A growl from my stomach reminded me that I hadn't eaten since breakfast, so I left her sitting there while I went into the kitchen to throw a couple of frozen pizzas into the oven.

When I came back into the living room to sit by Lucy, she gave me a serious look, a dark flush still on her face from the cold. "So what are you going to do about your dad?"

I sighed, not happy to be back on this subject. "Nothing, I guess. I promised Jason I would at least consider letting Alexondre teach me, but . . . "

Lucy cocked her head slightly. "His name is Alexondre?"

I nodded, waiting for her reaction.

"But . . . why would your mom give you a name so close to his? You would think after he left her alone and pregnant, she wouldn't want any reminders of him."

I shrugged. "Your guess is as good as mine. I still haven't decided whether or not to tell my mom that he's back, but if I want to ask her about my name, I'll have to tell her I met him."

Lucy shook her head slowly. "Too weird."

"Tell me about it. Now what's the plan for Lela?" I glanced at the grandfather-style wall clock that hung above where the TV used to be. It had luckily survived the TV's death with only minor scorching. It was just past 6:30.

Lucy's gaze followed mine to the clock. "I dunno. Just hear her out I guess. Max should be here soon. He wanted to be here before Lela."

A knock sounded at my front door. Speak of the devil.

"Come in!" I called.

Max opened the door and came striding in, shutting it gently behind him. He shucked off his light blue fleece to reveal a long-sleeved orange and yellow plaid shirt over faded jeans. Max is only about 5'4", and his sandy blond hair, and pale green eyes, are complemented by skin that would be densely freckled if he lived somewhere with more sun. He came and squeezed between Lucy and me on the couch, then turned to Lucy. "So what's this all about? You were so cryptic on the phone."

Lucy shrugged. "I told you all that I know. She wanted us together before she'd say anything."

Max looked grumpy. He often reminded me of a sullen elf, though I'd never say it to his face. He looked back and forth between Lucy and me. "I don't like this. I don't understand why she's still in town."

I had no time to placate Max, because another knock sounded at the door. This time, I got up to answer it. I walked quickly to the front door and opened it, trying to put up a front of confidence. Lela was outside in dark-wash jeans and a lavender cable knit sweater, standing a few feet back from the door as if she was afraid that I'd attack her. Given our past, her chances were about fifty-fifty.

Lela has long dark hair like Lucy's, but Lela's is more dense and slightly wavy. I still couldn't quite place her ethnicity, but her deep olive skin and exotic eyes were gorgeous none-the-less, sparking jealousy in all members of the female persuasion wherever she went I'm sure. But she was tall and willowy like me, so I couldn't hate her entirely. We curve-challenged girls got to stick together.

Behind her stood a man I didn't know, looking slightly more confident than Lela. He had nondescript brown hair, cut close to his scalp, that blended into his tanned skin, only a few shades lighter than the hair. I placed him around Lela's age, which I guessed was 22 or 23, I had never gotten the chance to ask.

The stranger was wearing the universal bad-boy uniform: black leather jacket over white t-shirt, and black leather boots covered by faded jeans. He aimed a crooked flirtatious smile at me. I mistrusted him instantly.

I stepped back from the door and gestured for them to come inside, which they did after a moment's hesitation from Lela. I shut the door and left Lela and the mystery man standing while I cleared the wrapping paper and ribbons off the loveseat. I put them in a pile on the multicolored patchwork rug that dominates my living room floor. Lela stepped forward slowly.

I sat back on the couch with Max and Lucy and gestured to the loveseat. "Have a seat."

Lela walked around the far side of the loveseat and sat down, folding her delicate hands in her lap. She then proceeded to stare at said hands and not say a word. The man came to sit casually beside Lela, slumping in his seat as if he hadn't a care in the world.

I looked at Lela, confused. "Well?"

Lela finally met my eyes. "I have a proposition for the three of you."

A proposition? I had a feeling I wasn't going to like this. She had fallen silent again so I waved my hands in a 'go on' gesture.

Lela took a deep breath and let it out, her full lips trembling slightly. "I think we should form a pack."

"Really?" Max asked, at the same time as Lucy said, "What?"

I was too stumped to speak.

Lela elaborated. "If we have a pack, we'll be safe. If another rogue wolf like Dan comes through and tries to bother us, we can call the Pack Coalition for help."

"The Pack Coalition?" Lucy asked at the same time I asked, "We?"

Lela was gaining confidence as she spoke. "You remember Abel, Dan's old pack leader? Well, he's also the leader of the Western Pack Coalition. The leader or alpha of each pack attends three Coalition meeting per year. They get together and discuss any news or problems, confirm pack size, and fill out paperwork for any new pack members."

"How do you know all of this?" I asked.

Lela brought her gaze back to me. "I traveled to Utah to talk to Abel. I wanted to get my facts straight before I approached you."

Max squinted thoughtfully. "So, what you're saying is that if we form a pack, we're protected by this Coalition thingy?"

Lela nodded excitedly. "Pretty much. I mean, we gotta do our part too. We pay dues, and if a wolf comes into our area and needs help, we have to help them, just as they would have to help us if we were in their area, which leads me to Nick." She gestured to the smiling man beside her who gave me a sarcastic wave in return.

"I met him a few weeks ago in California, while I was on my way back here," Lela went on. "He's basically in the same situation as the rest of us: no pack, easy picking for any rogue wolf trying to recruit underlings."

"This all sounds great," Lucy announced with a smile, surprising me. "Ever since the Dan incident, I've been constantly looking over my shoulder for the next rogue wolf to come and try to take Max and me away."

Max was nodding excitedly. "I agree. I'm in."

Lela smiled from ear to ear, but there was something I still wasn't getting, and I had a feeling I didn't want to know the answer. "So why did you want to talk to me?"

Lela's smile faltered slightly. "Well . . . we need an alpha."

I raised my eyebrows. "And?"

"And we need you to be that alpha," she said quickly, still fearing my reaction. Hit someone in the head with a fireplace poker one time and they never get over it.

I closed my eyes in frustration. I had enough problems to deal with, demonic and otherwise. I did not need wolf ones. "Why can't one of you be the alpha?"

41

Before Lela could answer, the oven timer went off. I held up a finger to belay her answer further so I could get up and get the pizzas out of the oven. I left them on top of the stove and went back to sit in the living room again. As I sat, I twirled my hand to end palm up in Lela's direction, sarcastically signaling her to answer my question.

Lela shifted in her seat, looking slightly embarrassed. "We don't qualify as alphas. None of us is strong enough."

I huffed out my breath in confusion. "And I am? I'm not even a wolf!" I was up and standing in front of Lela before I even realized it. I made myself stop and take a deep breath to keep myself from losing control. My temper was beginning to get ridiculous. Just another wonderful thing I could thank my dad for.

Lela waited a moment for me to calm down before she continued in the soft type of voice that's perfect for talking to crazy people. I'd been hearing that voice a lot lately. "You killed Dan," she began, "who was technically a pack leader, even though he was rogue. It qualifies you."

"Max helped," I said weakly as I let myself drop back down onto the couch. Max had thrown a can of gasoline on Dan to prevent the fire I had started from going out.

Lela shook her head. "Abel credits the killing to you. He's the one that has to approve our alpha. He approved you."

"What about *Nick*?" I asked snarkily, causing his annoying smile to falter.

"Doesn't qualify," Lela answered matter-of-factly, ignoring Nick's annoyed expression. I had a feeling Nick didn't enjoy admitting that a girl might be more powerful than him.

Lucy and Max turned to me expectantly.

I took a deep breath. Best not to think it over too much. I'd only talk myself out of it, and if Max and Lucy thought this would make them safe, then I wanted it. "I'll do it."

Lela squealed and leapt off the loveseat onto the couch to hug me awkwardly. "Thank you," she whispered, and I realized she had started to cry. I couldn't blame her; she'd had a rough year.

I patted her back awkwardly, not really sure what to do. Finally, she pulled herself together and climbed off of me. She stood slowly, wiping at her eyes with the lavender sleeve of her sweater. "Mind if I use your bathroom?"

I forced a smile that was probably more of a grimace. "Sure. Down the hall, first door on the left." I pointed to show her the way.

As Lela started towards the bathroom, Lucy leaned across Max's lap to pull me into a hug, which pretty much forced Max to join the hugging too.

Lucy ended the hug and settled back into her seat and smiled. "I feel so much better. No more worrying." Lucy paused for a minute, then went on, "and thanks Xoe. I know you don't want to do this."

I felt the fake smile fall from my lips. No, I did not want to do this. "Let's not get too excited yet. We still have to find out what forming a pack actually entails."

Nick sat silently, taking it all in with a slightly bemused smile on his face. He obviously didn't know me very well to be so at ease. I met his smile with one of my own. "I'm not in the business of trusting people these days," I began. "and just so you know, if you betray me, I'll kill you." So it was an empty threat, but wiping that smile off his face brightened my mood considerably. And who really knew how empty it was? These days I was never sure of much, especially in concerns to myself.

Lela came back out of the bathroom as I was smiling sweetly at Nick. She sat back down on the loveseat. After taking in Nick's sick expression, she slowly turned to me. "I, um, have all of the paperwork for us to fill out. Then all we have to do is go to the next Coalition meeting. Normally only Xoe would need to go, but Abel wants us all there for the first time."

I hadn't had a chance to think about the Coalition meetings. "Where are the meetings held?"

Lela shrugged. "The Coalition chooses a different state for each meeting, so that some pack leaders don't have to travel more than others. The next one will be in Utah with Abel's pack."

I cringed. "So I have to travel to these meetings three times a year?"

Lela shook her head. "You can send a member of your pack as your proxy to two of them. You're only required to physically attend one meeting per year."

"But I'm not eighteen, can I even buy a plane ticket?"

"I've already started looking for a job. I'm willing to foot the bill for travel, and for pack dues. I'll buy the ticket for you. It's worth it for me."

Good to know. "When is the Utah meeting?"

"The end of January. I'm not sure of the exact date."

Okay, once a year I could handle. I had the travel money from Abel's payment, but I'd keep that to myself for now. I wanted as little involvement in all this as possible. Plus, going to a pack meeting was worse enough without having to pay for it. The only remaining problem was what to tell my mom so that she'd let me go. Lucy would have even more trouble than I would. I turned and raised my eyebrows at her.

Her eyes were pinched with worry. "I'll figure it out," she said, understanding my silent question.

I let it drop. I didn't think it likely that she'd 'figure it out,' but I couldn't stop her from trying. My thoughts were interrupted by another knock on the door.

I sighed heavily and got up to answer it, wondering who it could be now. I opened the door, then slammed it closed again. My dad was outside. A quick, loud knock sounded at the door again. I considered just walking away, but grudgingly re-opened it. I took in my dad for the second time in the day and in my life, waiting patiently in his pale green sweater and dark gray slacks. It had gotten dark, and the sweater was a little thin for how cold it was outside, but he seemed unfazed by it. I raised my eyebrows in question and waited for him to explain his presence.

"We need to talk," he said simply.

I sighed loudly, making sure he took in my exasperation. "Kinda busy right now . . . "

45

"This cannot wait," he replied sharply, brushing a strand of his blond hair out of his face in agitation. "You may be in danger."

I squared my body to face his defensively. "Are you threatening me?"

My dad sighed. "Not in the least, but we need to talk. *Now*."

I knew I was going to regret it, but I stood aside and gestured for him to come in. He gave a startled nod, as if he hadn't expected the invitation, then stepped into my house, leaving the door open behind him. He looked around my living room, as if he were taking in every little detail. His eyes stopped on Lucy, Max, Nick, and Lela. "These are your wolves?" he asked.

My eyes widened. "How did you know?"

He shrugged and said simply, "Abel is a friend."

I was becoming very tired of Abel. The wolves in my living room stayed where they were sitting and waited with identical expressions on their faces: mild curiosity, with an edge of tension in response to the possible danger. It still creeped me out to see Lucy this way.

I turned back to my dad. "What did you mean about me being in danger?" There, that sounded nice and steady. Xoe, large and in charge.

"Abel contacted me this morning to tell me of the possibility of you becoming a pack leader," he began. "He also informed me that several wolves throughout California have gone missing. One has been found dead. I did some research and found three other missing persons cases; two in California, and one in Oregon. Upon further investigation, I realized that all three were alleged supernaturals: two witches and a merperson."

"Well aren't you a regular Nancy Drew," I said snarkily.

"Pay attention Alexondra," he replied sharply. "We don't know who's doing this."

I cocked my head, thinking, but my brain wasn't letting me put two and two together. "What does this have to do with me?"

My dad rolled his eyes. "Someone is abducting, and likely killing, supernatural beings. They worked their way up California, and have now moved on to Oregon."

"And you don't know who's doing it?" I asked, trying to buy myself some time to think.

"If I knew," he said bluntly, "they would have already been stopped."

Before I could process what 'stopping' them implied, I was distracted by movement at the front door. "Alex?" a small voice questioned.

My dad and I both spun, seeking the source of the voice. My mom was standing in the doorway, dressed in her khaki trench coat and dark brown, low-heeled boots. As soon as my dad fully faced her, she dropped her purse and shopping bags to the ground and stood flabbergasted, jaw agape.

"Hello Libby," my dad said calmly, slightly bowing his head in greeting.

My mom stormed into the living room. "Get . . . out! Get out! Get out! Get out!"

My dad just stood there for a moment, then walked right out the front door, not loosing a single iota of his calm. He shut the front door gently behind him. My mom stared at the door, stunned. Lucy, Max, Nick and

Lela were glued to their seats, looking more like frightened lambs than big bad wolves.

My mom turned horrified eyes to me. "What was he doing here Xoe?"

"I'll explain in a minute," I answered. "Would you please wait upstairs for me?"

My mom nodded, acting more like a child than a mother, no arguing whatsoever. She must have been seriously freaked. I turned away as the sound of her boots clicked hurriedly up the stairs. The four wolves stood. Lucy came forward and gave me a quick hug. "We should go. We'll talk more later."

I nodded numbly. "I'll walk you out."

As we walked out of my house I saw that my dad was still waiting outside, haloed by my front porch light. With the light reflecting off his pale skin and hair, he looked like some sort of solemn angel, but I definitely knew better than that. The only car outside was my mom's, so Lela, Nick, and Max had all apparently walked to my house, or maybe Max had a ride, he lived several miles away. Whatever. The four of them walked together down the street towards Lucy's house, though where Max and Nick would go, I didn't know. I realized that I didn't know where Lela was staying either, then realized that, at the moment, I didn't really care.

My dad walked up to stand beside me while I watched them go. I stifled a shiver at the feeling of his presence beside me. Once again the only car outside was my mom's, so my dad had apparently walked too. Or maybe he just went 'poof' and appeared at my door. I was betting on the latter. I just couldn't picture him strolling down my quaint neighborhood street, plus his expensive loafers were definitely not meant for extended outdoor travel.

Once my friends were out of sight, he turned to regard me. "You need protection," he said.

I kept my eyes focused on the now empty dark street. "Since when do you care?" I asked tiredly.

Ignoring my question he spoke again. "You should refuse the Pack Leader position. You don't understand how wolves can be, what the meetings will be like. It's a very *different* type of society."

I shrugged in reply, not caring to have his opinion on the subject.

He was silent for several minutes. "I'll be sending someone to watch over you." With that, he walked a few steps towards the street. He spoke without turning to face me. "I didn't leave by choice you know." Then he really did go 'poof', well it was more of a whoosh, leaving a cloud of smoke in his wake. I wasn't even surprised. That tells you just how weird the past few months had been for me.

Chapter Five

I wasn't looking forward to what I had to do next, but my mom was waiting patiently for me upstairs. I stood alone in my driveway and debated whether or not I could just follow in the direction Lucy, Max, Nick, and Lela had gone. With a sigh, I turned dutifully on my heel and marched back into my house, locking the door behind me. I kept my forward momentum and marched straight upstairs and down the hall to my mom's room.

I stood and took a deep breath before I pushed her bedroom door open and stepped into the dark red and purple themed interior. She was curled up on her burgundy bedspread with her back to me, still in her beige trench coat. Her face was hidden by waves of her brown hair. I sat beside her on the bed and waited for her to speak.

"What's going on Xoe?" she asked without looking at me.

I paused before speaking. I had a feeling that it was a mistake to let her in on everything, but it would also make life a little less complicated. "There are some things you need to know, but I have one question first."

My mom rolled onto her other side and looked up at me with her honey brown eyes puffy from crying. She waited for the question, not saying anything.

Here goes. "Why am I named after him? If dad left before I was born, why would you give me a name so similar to his?"

My mom looked down at her bed and started tracing her finger across the subtle embroidery on her comforter. For a moment I thought she wasn't going to answer, then she finally replied, "I'll tell you the truth, then you'll tell me everything?"

I nodded, then realized my mom was so intent on her bedspread that she didn't notice. "Yes." I replied as I sat on the bed beside her.

My mom took in a deep breath and let it out. "Your dad didn't leave until shortly after your first birthday."

My jaw dropped. "What?"

My mom finally met my eyes. "And it wasn't his choice."

I crossed my arms and waited for her to elaborate.

She grabbed my hand, forcing it back down by my side. "It was in the early spring," she began. "I took you to the park, and your dad was going to meet us there. We were going to have a picnic. It was still pretty cold out, so we were the only ones there. I had you in your stroller and we were waiting near the parking lot for your dad to show up. There was a man and he . . . he ran up behind me and grabbed my purse." She paused, eyes staring as if she was seeing the scene played before her eyes. "I should have just let him take it," she said quickly. "But . . . I don't know why, I held on. He pushed your stroller over to distract me."

When she stopped speaking I squeezed her hand a little tighter and waited for her to go on.

After a shuddering breath, she continued, "Out of nowhere, your dad appeared. He hadn't pulled up in his car, he was just *there*. He righted the stroller and made sure you were okay. You had started crying as soon as your stroller was pushed over. Yet you stopped the second your dad got there, even before he picked the stroller up. You had been connected to your dad like that since birth. You never cried around him."

"What happened after dad got there?" I prompted, noticing her subtle attempt to end the story.

My mom was silent for a moment, her face completely blank. Finally she went on. "He went after the attacker. The man just stood gaping at your dad, probably wondering where he had come from. When the attacker realized your dad's intent, he turned to run, but your dad knocked him down and was just suddenly on him. I just watched. I didn't know what to do. Your dad wrapped his hands around the man's throat. I smelled this horrible burning smell."

Her voice had faded so that I could barely hear her. I had to lean my head right by her face to hear what she said next. "A few seconds later your dad stood and turned to face me. He told me not to look, but . . . the man's neck was just gone, reduced to ash."

"Ash?" I asked.

"Yeah," she mumbled. "I know it sounds crazy, but that's what I saw."

"What happened next?" I asked.

"I grabbed you out of your stroller and ran. It was stupid of me, but I didn't even put you in your car seat. I held you in my lap while I drove home, then I went inside and locked all of the doors, only to realize that your dad was already inside the house. He had somehow gotten there before me. I told him to get out, that I never wanted to see him again. He had killed a man. Your dad left, but he said he'd come back once I had calmed down. As soon as he was gone, I packed a few things, took you, and left." She took another shuddering breath. "Today was the first time I've seen him since that day."

"So you left him because he killed a guy?" I prompted.

She breathed in and seemed to mentally gather herself before she explained. "That was only part of it. I mean, I was of course horrified by that fact, but I also feared the consequences of your dad's actions. What if there was an investigation? A dead man in a park with his throat burnt away would raise more than a few eyebrows. Plus, I had to wonder what else your dad had done that I didn't know about. Maybe if it was just me I would have stayed to find out, but I felt I was protecting you."

Okay, I just had to ask. "What did the police think…you know, when they found the body?"

My mom shrugged. "I checked the papers for months. The body was never found. That fact alone helped me stay strong in my decision."

I raised my eyebrows in question.

"Your dad must have gotten rid of the body," she explained. "He could have covered up so many other things. I'm not sure I really ever knew him at all."

I cringed thinking of the Dan incident. I couldn't really throw stones at someone for being involved in covering up a murder.

Not noticing my reverie, my mom wrapped up her explanation. "And that's it, that's why you never knew your father. As time passed I stopped thinking about him as much. I aimed all of my attention on you."

It was a lot to take in, but it made sense. I finally knew why my dad had left us, or, I guess, why we left him. "Were you guys married?" I asked.

"No. We had planned on it. We had a date set and everything."

"Oh," I replied.

My mom sat up and leaned her back against her headboard, then put her arm around my shoulders and drew me over to sit right beside her. She gave her body a shake and settled back in, as if casting away the residue of her past experience. Wish I could do that.

"Now," my mom said, "your turn."

"Okay," I began, "not really sure where to start."

"Start with why your dad was here. He is gone, isn't he?"

I laughed. "Yeah, he's gone, for now."

My mom let out a nervous chuckle. "Good. Now explain."

I turned toward my mom to give her direct eye contact, so she'd know I was serious. "Dad's a demon."

My mom squinted her eyes in confusion. "I'll admit, the man has his faults, but calling him a demon is a little harsh. I've come to terms with the fact that what he did to that man, he did to protect us. Even if I can't fully accept what he did, I know why he did it."

I sighed. "No. I mean he's actually a demon, like a magical . . . being."

My mom raised her eyebrows at me skeptically, but her eyes were uncertain. Her face slowly fell into worried lines. "The combusting appliances?" she asked.

I nodded my head and pointed a finger at my chest. "Half-demon."

"I don't understand," she replied. "I mean I do," she went on. "I of course always suspected something of your dad, ever since that day. But a demon? Like from Hell?"

I shook my head. "I don't know the exact details of where demons come from, but think less like Heaven and Hell, and more like legends and monsters."

My mom's shoulders slumped as she looked away from my eyes. "I'm gonna need some time to think about this."

I almost left it at that, but I figured it would be better to get it all out now . . . better for me at least. "There's more."

My mom whipped her head around to face me again. "More?" she asked, surprised.

Okay, just had to say it all, then get out. She could deal with the information how she wanted. She'd just have to get over it . . . ri-ght. "Lucy and Max are werewolves," I said quickly. "And Jason's a vampire. Okay bye." I got up to rush for the door, then realized that my mom hadn't let go of my hand.

She yanked me back to the bed. "*What* did you say?"

I smiled nervously and tried in vain to free my hand.

My mom turned frightened eyes to me. "Are they . . . dangerous?"

"No," I answered quickly, then corrected myself, "well, not really. Not any more dangerous than I am."

"Now," she began, "when you say, um, *vampire,* what do you mean?"

I shrugged. "Like, well, I actually mean vampire. Think Dracula with a few minor tweaks."

My mom lifted her free hand to press against her eyes. "I don't see how that's possible. I mean, you and your . . . father are just like humans with a little something extra, but a vampire? I've seen him in sunlight, and he doesn't look like a dead guy."

I squirmed a bit at that. I didn't like to think of Jason as a dead guy. Me squeamish? Never. "Well, he did kinda die," I explained, "but it's not like he's actually dead, and he has no problem being in sunlight."

My mom suddenly removed her hand from her eyes and turned to face me. "*Please* tell me that he doesn't drink your blood."

I cringed, yet another thing I didn't like to think about in regards to Jason. "Animal blood actually," I corrected.

My mom cringed in return. "Well *that's* reassuring. Have you ever seen him drink it?"

I shook my head, confused. "I'd rather not."

"Well then how do you know he's a vampire?" She countered.

Oh. I sighed. She was in the second stage of denial; grasping at straws. "He is," I confirmed.

My mom's face crumpled back into worried lines. "And . . . werewolves? How can little Lucy be a werewolf?"

"She got scratched," I replied matter-of-factly.

"By what, er, um, who?" she asked skeptically.

"It's not important," I blurted. "He's gone now."

"Define 'gone,'" my mom ordered.

"He's *gone,*" I said with meaning.

My mom shook her head quickly. "Nevermind. I don't want to know. Is that everything?"

I breathed a sigh of relief. "Yeah, that's all."

She loosened her grip on my hand and stared off into space. "Okay. I'm going to have more questions, but that's about all I can take for now," she said numbly. "We'll talk more later."

I got up to leave, but paused at the door and turned to face my mom again. "I, um, still have some pain killers from when I broke my arm. I didn't really use them, but they're supposed to knock you out pretty good . . . "

My mom raised an eyebrow, lending expression to her otherwise blank stare. "Why didn't you take them?"

"Um," I began, not really sure how to explain. "I kind of healed a little faster than I let on."

My mom's mouth formed into a little *o* of understanding.

"So, do you want them?" I asked again.

She kept her gaze straight ahead and answered, "Yes please."

Chapter Six

As soon as my mom was dead to the world, I headed to my room, utterly exhausted. What a day.

I opened my bedroom door to find Jason patiently waiting on my bed. I walked in, shutting the door behind me, then plopped down beside him on my dark green comforter. As soon as I sat, I let my back fall to the bed, swinging my arms over my head with an exaggerated sigh. Jason followed suit.

We had been lying silently with our legs hanging off the bed, and that's a lot of legs, with me at 5'8", and Jason at 6'2". Suddenly Jason spoke, "I saw Brian outside."

"And?" I prompted. Brian was my next-door neighbor after all, there was nothing unusual about seeing him, and Jason knew I didn't like to talk about him.

"He said you were with some guy that disappeared into thin air."

"That was my dad," I answered. "So Brian actually talked to you?"

"Yes," he answered plainly, but didn't go on.

"Well?" I urged. "What else did he say?"

Jason cleared his throat uncomfortably. "He said to keep that weird stuff behind closed doors."

"Why that little . . . " I began.

"What else has happened since I left you at Lucy's?" Jason interrupted.

He was right to interrupt. I had to avoid getting mad . . . for now. Once I had control of my powers though, Brian had a thing or two comin'. I pushed Brian to the back of my mind and gathered my thoughts to explain things to Jason.

I took in a deep breath. This would be a long speech. "Well, Lela's still in town, along with another werewolf, which has somehow resulted in me becoming the leader of a werewolf pack. My dad, as you know, showed up at my front door, shortly followed by my mom, who, of course, was a bit shocked. My dad says that we're all in danger, because someone is abducting and killing supernatural beings. And I finally had to fill my mom in on everything. Well, everything except the possibility of abduction. She's got enough to worry about already."

Jason turned his head towards me and raised his eyebrows. "You told her *everything*?"

I nodded my head, making my hair go static-y from my bedspread. "Yep, all about my werewolf pack, vampire boyfriend, and demon dad."

Jason cringed. "Does she hate me know?"

I shrugged, not able to care too much right at that moment. "She was kind of in shock I think. Only time will tell how she's going to take everything."

Jason nodded, then grabbed my hand and gave it a tight squeeze. "And she never knew what your dad was?"

"Well, she suspected something, and that reminds me of my other news. My mom always told me that my dad left before I was born. Turns out, he stayed past my first birthday, and he didn't choose to go. My mom and I left him. Of course, I still hate him. He could have at least tried to find us, rather than just accepting my mom's decision." I hesitated and glanced at Jason when I realized I was babbling.

I scooted over to lay my head on Jason's chest and he wrapped his arm around me obligingly. "You have had quite a day," he said softly.

I sighed. "Tell me about it."

Jason chuckled softly and began stroking my hair. "Now, how on earth have you become the leader of a wolf pack?"

I got started on that confusing explanation, including a brief rant on the existence of Nick. We talked things over for several hours, then at some point I fell asleep. I woke up underneath my comforter with my head on one of my yellow pillows. I could feel the press of Jason's body against my back. "Morning," he said, as he sensed that I was awake.

Jason doesn't sleep. It's a vampire thing. He stays over a lot (unbeknownst to my mom), and usually lies with me all night. I once asked him if he ever got bored and he admitted that I talk in my sleep a lot. I let the subject drop before he could tell me all of the likely embarrassing things I say.

I rolled over to face him. "I better check on my mom."

He nodded. "I am going to stop by my apartment. Do you want me to come back afterwards?"

"Well duh." I answered, and before I knew it, he had kissed my cheek and was out the window. I realized I was still dressed in my burgundy sweater and jeans, with my hair plastered to the side of my head. I decided to take a quick shower before I faced my mom again.

Once I had dried off and fixed my hair, I dressed in black jeans and a long-sleeved v-neck shirt that was so dark a shade of blue, it almost matched the jeans. My clothes represented my mood perfectly.

I walked out of my room and down the hall to my mom's door. I knocked once.

No answer.

"Mom?" I called.

Still no answer.

I waited a moment more, then twisted the knob and walked in. My mom's bed was made and she was nowhere to be seen. I left her room and went downstairs to check the rest of the house. Empty. Her car was gone from the driveway.

There was a half-pot of coffee waiting for me in the kitchen. I gratefully filled a cup up and took a sip. It tasted burnt, letting me know it had been made hours ago. I sat at the pale wood dining room table and sipped my burnt coffee, not really sure whether or not I should be worried. She had taken her car, so it was hopefully safe to say that no one had taken her. Then it dawned on me. Duh, she had gone to work. I was so preoccupied with worry about how she would act today, that I completely forgot that she'd be at work.

Laughing over my stupidity, I got up and made some toast with butter and orange marmalade, then sat back down to wait for Jason. After a few minutes, I heard the crunch of tires on the gravel of my driveway, and got up to let Jason in. I smiled as I opened the door to see him standing there in faded jeans, green flannel shirt, and hiking boots. He could clean up quite nicely when the need arose, but outdoor casual was his normal mode of dress. I gave him a quick kiss hello, then led him back to the dining room table so I could finish my toast.

"You want anything to eat?" I asked as we sat down.

He shook his head. "I ate at my apartment, thanks."

I briefly wondered what he had eaten. I knew that he had to drink animal blood occasionally to survive, but I had never thoroughly discussed it with him. I was fine with not having the details on that unsettling tidbit.

"Where is your mom?" He asked.

"Work," I answered casually, as if I had known all along.

He opened his mouth in an *o* of realization. Apparently he had forgotten too. He quickly schooled his expression and cleared his throat to hide his lack of foresight. "What is on our agenda today?"

"Well," I began between bites of toast. "I'm assuming Lela will be back sometime today with the paperwork I need to fill out. She seemed pretty anxious to get the ball rolling. And unfortunately, I'm sure my dad and/or his proxy will show up at some point."

Jason raised his eyebrows in question. "Proxy?"

I nodded, then spoke around another bite of toast. "Yeah, he said he'd be sending someone to *watch over me*." I wiggled my fingers in mock spookiness.

Jason gave me his crooked half-smile. "Sounds ominous."

I nodded while I took a sip of bitter coffee. "Tell me about it."

"So all we have to do is wait?" he asked.

"Or," I smiled mischievously. "We could go hiking, and ignore all of the impending doom."

Jason put out his hand for me to shake. "You have got yourself a deal."

I shook his hand then got up to take my plate and empty coffee mug to the kitchen sink. I left a note for my mom by the phone, just in case she came home for lunch. Then I went to sit by the backdoor to swap my sneakers in for my worn in, dark brown hiking boots. As I was lacing up my boots I could hear Jason rummaging through my kitchen for some snacks to bring with and I smiled. Avoiding responsibility is so much more fun when you have someone to conspire with. Hopefully we could make it an all day hike.

Jason walked towards me as I stood up from tying my shoes, his hand and arms full of snacks and a several bottles of water. I took my dark green hiking backpack off of the hook on the wall and held it open for him to dump everything into. The backpack was already equipped with first aid equipment and pepper spray, so we were ready to go. I guess if an enemy were willing to take on a vampire and a half-demon, they probably wouldn't hesitate at the sight of pepper spray, but it still made me feel safe. Ridiculous, but true.

Jason took the backpack from me and swung it over his shoulder as we walked out the backdoor. I locked the door behind us, then made Jason stand still so I could put my keys into the backpack.

We started up the trail that begins shortly after my backyard ends, and I instantly felt better. Like magic, the woods took custody of the weight of all of my predicaments. Sadly, they would be waiting for me when I got back.

Jason turned to me as we walked up the path. "Which trail do you want to take?"

Shelby is full of hiking trails, three of which stem right from my backyard, though you could access them from other paths. "Waterfalls?" I asked.

Jason nodded merrily and took the trail that led off to the left. It was my favorite trail. It led up to a series of waterfalls. Not like, big rainforest type of waterfalls, more the type you find along a babbling brook. The waterfalls are near the stone remnants of several old, dirt-floor houses. They basically just form partial walls now, the roofs long-since disintegrated.

We walked in a comfortable silence, birdsong and the distant running water the only sounds to accompany our footsteps. As we walked farther uphill, the trail became more narrow and the trees more dense. The trail up to the waterfalls isn't used very often, don't ask me why. I guess people just didn't know about it.

It took us about an hour to reach the first of the old houses. It was a mile or so below the waterfalls and the other less dilapidated houses. Jason went and sat on one crumbled wall that was little more than a few stones stacked on top of each other, and gestured for me to sit

65

beside him. As I sat he swung the backpack off of his shoulder to dig out the water bottles. He turned to me with a fake smile plastered on his face and I immediately knew that something was wrong. His eyes scanned our surroundings as he faced me. "Don't look now," he said almost inaudibly, "but someone's watching us."

I, of course, immediately turned my head in search of our anonymous watcher. I caught movement from the corner of my eye as someone ducked behind a bush about thirty feet away from where we were sitting. Jason gave my knee a squeeze, then slowly rose to investigate.

I tried to pretend that nothing was happening, and started rummaging through the backpack until my fingers wrapped around my pepper spray. Once again, yes, I am a half-demon and shouldn't need pepper spray, but my powers aren't exactly reliable, so pepper spray it was.

I watched Jason out of the corner of my eye as he walked slowly to where I had seen the movement. He walked casually amongst the trees with his hands clasped behind his back. Just a harmless human strolling through the woods. Ri-ight.

The scuffle sounded again to my right. It was getting closer to me. Jason turned his head at the sound and changed his course to head towards it. I stood and began to approach the area where the scuffle had sounded, with the intention of trapping who or whatever it was between Jason and me.

My heart pounded in my ears as we both drew closer to the cluster of bushes where we thought the sound had come from. I stopped a few feet away from the first bush and waited for Jason to catch up. He looked irritated that I had involved myself in the situation. A bit over-protective at times, was my Jason.

Suddenly, a man leapt from where he had been crouching several feet to the right of where I had been looking. I caught a glimpse of a green jacket and dark hair before he turned on his heel to run away through the woods.

Jason whooshed by me in a blur of motion, hot on the man's heels. I blinked slowly, shocked at how fast it had all happened, then set off in the direction Jason had gone, pepper spray gripped tightly in one sweaty palm.

I had already lost sight of the man as well as Jason, so I was basically running blind. The trees in the area were so dense that I couldn't see more than twenty feet ahead of me. Knowing that there was no way that I'd catch up to Jason, especially with all the roots and vegetation I was tripping on, I veered left towards the trail. Hopefully the un-obscured path would allow me to catch up.

After several more minutes of stumbling through the dense forest, I reached the narrow trail leading back down the mountain. I hurled myself forward, despite the burning sensation building in my lungs. I continued sprinting down the trail for what seemed like a good ten minutes, but was probably only about three, until I finally had to stop and catch my breath. I hunched over with my hands on my knees and tried to suck in enough air. I couldn't hear anything over the pounding of my heart.

I crouched down into a squat to wait. It had been stupid of me to take a chance and veer from the direction

Jason had taken. Now he could be anywhere, left to fight our nameless watcher on his own. I stood up and decided to cut through the woods to my right, then make my way back to where I had left my backpack. The going was much slower when avoiding trees, so if I was lucky and they hadn't passed me, I might run into them on my way up.

I stumbled along through the vegetation, feeling increasingly unsure
of my choice to go back. It would probably have made more sense to go home and call the police, but if our watcher was something supernatural, it was better to not get them involved.

There is an unspoken rule for supernatural beings. It's mainly governed over by the werewolves since they're the most organized. It states that supernatural matters are to be handled within the supernatural community. There are the occasional slip-ups that often result in sensational news stories, but for the most part, we keep things quiet.

My legs still burned from all of the running and my pace began to lag as I navigated my way through the trees. All I could see was quiet, moist vegetation and damp earth where the sun couldn't penetrate the trees. I noticed that my hiking boot was untied. I crouched down in the damp soil on one knee to tie it. I began to reach for the laces, then paused as the sound of hurried footsteps thudded towards me. I turned just in time to see our nameless watcher, who was looking back over his shoulder as he ran.

I tried to stand and move out of the way, but my reaction was too slow, and he barreled right into me. We both went flying downhill in a tangled mass. We rolled a few times, each of us trying to pin the other. I couldn't for the life of me remember how to burn him. I'd only burned someone once before, and that had been an accident. The one I lit on fire hadn't exactly been accidental, but I still had no idea how I'd done it.

I had lost my pepper spray somewhere during our fall and cursed my bad luck. I struggled in the mud and leaves against him, realizing in horror that he was gaining the upper hand. His greater weight continued to his advantage as he finally managed to pin my arms to the ground while he straddled me to hold my body down. He was obviously something other than human, or else I would have been able to put up more of a fight.

I got my first good look at his face as I struggled to free myself. He had slightly wavy hair that was almost black. If fell in front of his eyes, that at the moment, looked dark gray as he got a more secure grip on my wrists. A strong nose that was almost too prominent complemented his light olive skin, thin, but not too thin mouth, and angular jaw line.

He glared at me angrily. "Stop struggling," he spoke with a slight accent that I couldn't place. "I'm not here to hurt you."

I assessed the situation, then I went limp and smiled, because I remembered something that he had apparently forgotten. The man gave me a confused look, surprised that I had given up so easily, then Jason came flying out of nowhere and knocked the man off me. I got kneed in the gut as they tumbled away. Jason and the man began to fight for the upper hand, kicking up mud and leaves much in the same way that I had just experienced.

Meanwhile, I stayed curled up on the ground trying to get a full breath in.

Finally I was able to stand, and I immediately turned my attention to the ongoing struggle. "Freeze!" I shouted.

Both men turned to regard me with identical expressions: angry, and a little confused, since they had apparently forgotten me. Jason had our watcher in an only partially effective headlock. Both of them were covered in mud and dry leaves and I realized that I was too.

I quickly brushed myself off then looked the man in his dark gray eyes. "What do you want?"

He tried again to break Jason's hold on his neck, then gave up with a sigh and regarded me. "I was only supposed to follow you. I didn't expect you to chase me."

I crossed my arms and gave him an impatient expression. "And why were you following me?"

"Your dad asked me to," he answered angrily.

I should have known. He just couldn't leave well enough alone. I turned my attention to Jason. "Let him go?"

Jason did as I asked. The man stood and brushed off his jeans and green military surplus jacket. Jason stood up next, obviously favoring his right leg. I felt a pang of worry at the thought that he might be injured, then mentally corrected myself. Jason wouldn't think twice about a sprained ankle, he was a vampire after all.

Jason gave the man a vengeful look and asked, "What are you?"

The man ignored Jason and shuffled towards me, holding out his hand. "My name's Chase."

I ignored his offered hand. "He didn't ask who you are. He asked what you are."

The man, Chase, smiled pleasantly at me. "It's none of his business what I am."

I sighed. I was tired of this. "So my dad sent you to keep an eye on me because of the abductions?"

Chase nodded, but didn't elaborate any further.

I was tired. My legs hurt. I had plenty of new bumps and bruises, and on top of it all, my clothes were completely ruined. I was so over this. I picked up my pepper spray that I had spotted during our odd conversation, marched up to Jason and grabbed his hand, then started off in the direction of the trail. Chase caught up to walk on my other side, at least as well as he could in between avoiding trees. I ignored him.

Life had finally gotten back to normal, as normal as it could get given my situation. Now in the course of a day, I had become a werewolf pack leader, and I suddenly had a dad again, a dad that was interfering way too much for my liking.

We reached the trail and I looked longingly in the direction of my home. I guess this was what I got for avoiding my new pack leader responsibilities. I decided to abandon my backpack and hope that it would still be there tomorrow. I just wanted to go home.

No one spoke the entire way to my house. We cut across my yard to my backdoor and I grimaced, only then realizing that I had left my keys in my backpack. I crouched to get the key from underneath one of our many lawn gnomes. Now that Chase knew where it was

I would have to hide it somewhere else. Or maybe I would just keep it on me. I looked at the man standing patiently on my left. He was around 6', a little shorter than Jason. He had his hands in his pockets and was rocking back and forth on his heels like a little kid. Yeah, there was no way I was putting the key back in my yard.

Without saying a word, I unlocked the door, let Jason go in ahead of me, then shut it as soon as I had walked in, leaving Chase outside. He hadn't seemed surprised.

The house was dark and quiet, letting me know that my mom still wasn't home. I went to the little dark wood table that stands in my living room beside the entrance to the kitchen to check the answering machine. The little red light was flashing so I pushed the play button. As Lucy's voice filtered out, Jason brushed by me into the kitchen, letting his hand trail across my back as he walked.

Lucy's voice said that her and Max were meeting Lela and Nick at Irvine's pizza parlor tonight to fill out paperwork, and to call her back and let her know if I could come. I pushed the button to erase Lucy's message as Jason came back out of the kitchen.

I looked a question at his angry, furrowed brow.

Jason glanced in the direction of my kitchen window, then back to me. "He is sitting on your porch swing. He is *humming*."

I raised my eyebrows. "Humming?"

Jason nodded. "It sounds like Beethoven's 5th."

Jason walked towards my couch and I followed, thinking that Beethoven's 5th was an odd thing to hum. Jason and I both slumped onto the couch. I felt like I had run a marathon. I leaned my head back against the couch cushion.

Jason spoke without looking at me. "He smells like you."

"So Chase is a demon?" I asked.

"At least half," he replied. "Maybe more. He has less of a human smell than you do."

I nodded, not wanting to discuss Chase any further. "I left my keys in the backpack"

Jason glanced at me, then leaned his head back against the cushion. "I will go get it." He stood to leave.

I stopped him with a raised hand. "Lucy wants to meet at Irvine's tonight."

Jason nodded without looking at me. He seemed as exhausted as I was. "I will retrieve the backpack, then I will go with you."

I nodded as Jason turned to go. I didn't want to go to Irvine's. I didn't want to fill out the paperwork that would make me a pack leader. I didn't want to go outside and deal with Chase.

If there's one thing I've learned, you can't always get what you want.

Chapter Seven

While Jason was gone, I changed out of my dirty clothes. It was lucky that I had chosen to wear dark colors. Maybe the mud stains wouldn't show after all. I dressed in dark wash jeans and a deep purple turtleneck and went back downstairs to call Lucy.

The phone rang only once before a sharp voice answered, "Hello?"

"This is Xoe," I responded. "Is Lucy home?"

Silence on the other end of the line. After a minute Lucy picked up.

I sighed loudly to show her my exasperation. "What time?"

"In thirty minutes. You need a ride? Lela's picking me and Allison up."

"Jason's taking me, so I'll meet you there."

"Thanks again Xoe, I mean it."

"Yeah, yeah," I said sarcastically, then hung up the phone.

As soon as the phone clicked in the cradle it dawned on me that Allison had no reason to be there. It was likely that she'd try and include herself in the whole werewolf pack thing. She hates being left out. I guess I'd find out in thirty minutes.

Jason came clambering in through the backdoor a moment later. It still astounded me how fast he could be. Supposedly I should have been able to move that fast too, but the supernatural speed thing was beyond me. I listened as he rummaged through the backpack to find my keys. He came into the living room and tossed them to me. "Ready to go?" he asked. "I still need to stop by my apartment and change."

I smiled despite my foul mood. Jason always made me smile, even when he was being sullen and pouty. What might have been annoying from someone else, I found enduring coming from Jason. Xoe, big bad half-demon, going soft. "We're supposed to meet them in thirty minutes."

He walked up and put his arm around my shoulders. "Let us go and face your little fiend . . . I mean friend."

I held up a finger. "Correction, let us go and ignore my little friend."

Jason smiled and walked me to the front door. We both went outside, locking the door behind us, then headed straight for Jason's charcoal gray sports car. Chase watched us from his seat on my porch swing, then got up and jogged after us. "Where are you going?" he called.

I continued ignoring him as I waited for Jason to walk to the driver's side and unlock the doors.

Chase caught up to stand beside me. "If you won't tell me, I'm going to have to call your dad."

I still couldn't place his accent, Greek maybe? "Seriously?" I asked.

He nodded, and grinned from ear to ear when he realized that he had me. Man he was annoying.

I sighed and gestured to the backseat. "Get in."

Jason gave me a startled expression over the roof of his car.

I shrugged. "I'd rather deal with him than my dad."

Jason still looked skeptical as he unlocked the doors and got in. I slid into the front passenger's seat and buckled my seatbelt, then turned with a squeak of leather to look back at Chase as Jason pulled out of my driveway. "So what, he just told you to stick with me and make sure I don't get abducted?"

Chase nodded. He was still in his muddy jeans and green jacket, which he had unzipped to reveal a black t-shirt.

"And how is it that you know my dad?" I asked when he didn't elaborate further.

He glanced at Jason, then back to me. "We can discuss that later."

I took my turn glancing at Jason, who was pretending to ignore our conversation, then turned my eyes back to Chase. "You know I'll just tell him later." I said.

Chase crinkled his nose in irritation. "That is your choice, but the fact remains that it is none of his business." He was silent for a moment, and I started to turn around to face forward. "So where are we going?" he added casually.

I stopped my turn long enough to smile sweetly at him and mimic, "That is simply none of your business."

I finished turning forward, still smiling. I watched out of the corner of my eye as a small smile crept across Jason's face to match my own.

Sara C. Roethle

A few minutes later, we pulled into the parking lot of Jason's apartment complex and parked in one of the many vacant spaces. It was one of the nicer apartment complexes in Shelby (which isn't saying much, since it's one of only three). He could afford it with the money he had made tracking down and aiding in the "disposal" of Dan. I knew he'd have to take another job sometime soon. The money couldn't last forever, especially now that I'd found out he only got half of what I did, but I tried not to think about it.

Jason turned off the ignition and glanced at me, obviously not wanting to leave me alone in the car with Chase. I gave him a subtle nod, letting him know that I could handle things, and he reluctantly exited the car and went up the concrete stairs to his apartment.

Without the car heater I began to shiver despite my turtleneck. Normally Jason would have left the car running for me, but I couldn't blame him for being preoccupied. I looked out at the dreary cold streets to a couple walking in heavy winter coats. Okay, so maybe I could blame him just a little.

Chase stuck his head up beside my shoulder. "You want my jacket?" he asked. "It's a little dirty . . . "

I shook my head and answered quickly, "I'm fine." Why, oh why didn't I bring a jacket?

"You sure?" Chase prompted.

I nodded, not wanting to take his jacket on sheer principle.

"Suit yourself," Chase replied as he leaned back into his seat and began humming. This time it sounded like Depeche Mode's *Enjoy the Silence*.

78

Jason finally came trotting back down the stairs to rescue me, dressed in jeans and a navy sweater. He slid back into the driver's seat and quickly started the car to blast the heat. He looked at me with an embarrassed smile. "Sorry," he apologized.

"No worries," I grumbled as we pulled out to head to Irvine's.

Irvine's is one of the many mediocre pizza parlors in town. There are a few quality ones, but we always went to Irvine's, don't ask me why. After we parked, we walked straight into the brightly lit pizza parlor to get out of the cold.

Irvine's is decorated to look like a retro diner complete with jukebox and red vinyl booths and stools. Lucy and the others were nowhere to be seen, so we slid into one of the large corner booths to wait. Jason slid in to sit on one side of me as Chase went around to the other end of the booth to slide in on my other side. I sat awkwardly with my hands in my lap and longed for the night to be over.

We ordered two extra-large pizzas and a few pitchers of soda as we waited. Finally Lela came striding through the door looking long and lean in all black with a stack of papers hugged to her chest. Lucy, Max, and Allison strode in shortly after her, all smartly dressed in heavy winter coats. Lela spotted us instantly and came clacking up in her high-heeled black boots. She slid in beside Chase, never questioning his presence. Lucy and Max slid in after her.

Allison paused in front of the table and gave Chase a less than friendly look. "Who are you?"

Chase gave her a stoic expression and stared back.

"This is Chase," I answered tiredly.

Allison slid in next to Jason, flipping her long honey-blonde hair irritably, and grumbling something about a "rude, pretentious, slimeball," or something of that nature.

I was surprised at Allison's attitude. She usually took any opportunity she could to meet a new cute boy. I had a feeling it had something to do with her feeling left out lately. She was the only human left in the group, and now there was another presumably non-human guy taking up more of her friend time. And who said I wasn't perceptive?

"Where's Nick?" I asked.

"Who cares?" Allison grumbled.

"He said he'd meet us here," Lela answered over her.

The waitress came out of the kitchen with a pizza gripped in each of her hands. She set them on our table and promised to be right back with plates. Tension eased inside of me as the smell of cheese and mushrooms wafted up from the pizzas.

Lela waited long enough for the waitress to bring our plates, then got right down to business. She handed Lucy and Max their forms and I let out a sigh of relief when I saw that they were only a few pages thick. Then she handed me my forms. I gaped at the stack of papers in my hands. It was a friggin' book! I turned to Lela with my jaw agape. "Seriously?" I asked incredulously.

She had the courtesy to look abashed. "Sorry Xoe, the only information the coalition really cares about is that of the pack leader."

I sighed and set the packet down on the table and took the offered pen from Lela. I grabbed my first slice of pizza with my left hand and began filling out my basic information with my right. Chase seemed to be taking things in stride, so I assumed my dad had filled him in on everything. He sat perfectly at ease as he devoured his first slice of pizza and ignored everyone. Jason was sitting closer to me than was necessary, and I was beginning to feel more than a little overwhelmed.

Nick showed up a few minutes after the pizza, and had to pull up a chair to sit at the edge of the table that wasn't surrounded by the booth. Lela smiled and handed him a stack of papers. I began to go back to my paperwork, but something made me take a second look at Lela's smile. Nick had looked down to his paperwork, but Lela continued to smile all googly-eyed at him. Oh man, she totally liked him. It made me trust him even less. Not because she liked him, but perhaps her judgment of him was clouded, and her judgment was all we had to go on in trusting him. I looked back down to my paperwork, feeling even more uneasy, if that was even possible.

By the time I had finished my second slice, Lucy, Max, and Nick had finished their forms and handed them back to Lela. I was still working on mine, and the questions were becoming more and more strange the further I got. Was it really necessary for them to know my blood type? Plus, I was entirely at a loss as to what I should put under the section labeled "preferred hunting grounds."

Allison cleared her throat and gave me a meaningful look when I glanced at her. She and Lucy both excused themselves to go to the bathroom. Catching on, I got up and followed them. So it was terribly obvious that we wanted to talk amongst ourselves, could you really blame us? The three of us walked into the bathroom and shut the door firmly behind us.

After checking that all of the stalls were empty, Allison whirled on me and asked, "Who is that other guy and why is he here?"

I turned to Lucy. "I assume you filled her in on the stuff with my dad?"

Lucy nodded and I turned back to Allison. "Chase is my dad's idea of a bodyguard."

"Because of the abductions?" Lucy asked.

I nodded. "Yep, Jason and I caught him watching us in the woods."

Allison frowned. "Why is he still with you?"

Lucy answered for me, already seeing my logic. "It's him or your dad?"

I nodded again as I turned to push open the door. "Yep, the lesser of two evils."

Allison pursed her lips. "I don't like it."

I stopped in mid-motion and smiled wanly. "Neither do I, but Chase is the least of our worries right now."

Allison nodded her head in agreement. "I don't think the pack thing is a good idea."

That wasn't what I was expecting. I turned to fully face her again and cocked my head, waiting for her to explain her logic.

"It's just . . . " she began, then took a moment to consider her words. I noticed the chagrined expression on Lucy's face and deduced that they had already discussed this. "It seems like a big commitment," Allison went on. "You have to fill out all of these forms, and promise to meet with all of these people you don't know, and then there's Nick. How can we even begin to trust *him*? He came out of nowhere."

I shrugged. "What else can we do?"

"That's just it," Allison continued. "It seems like there's never any choice on anything. You have no choice but to let that Chase guy hang around, you have no choice but to form a pack. There should be choices."

I was getting a headache. I met Lucy's tired expression, identical to my own when I answered, "I agree, but there aren't."

Allison stomped her foot to bring attention back to herself. "How can you two be so calm about everything!"

Finally getting angry, I raised my voice, "Stop it Al! I can't help what I am, or who my dad is, and Lucy couldn't help being scratched by Dan. We're just trying to make the best of our situations."

"I know that!" Allison yelled back, her face becoming increasingly flushed. "But you should be upset about it!"

I began to shout back, but forced myself to stop. Getting angry in a public place was *so* not a good idea. I knew I should be understanding of Allison being upset, but there was only so much I could take. When it came down to it, Allison was upset because Lucy and I had problems, but *we* were the ones that actually had to deal with the problems. If dealing with them meant accepting things, then so be it.

Lucy reached for Allison to calm her down just as Lela peeked her head into the bathroom. "Everything all right?" she asked.

"Peachy," Allison snapped, before stomping out of the bathroom past Lela. I gave Lucy a sad smile and we both followed her out.

Once we were back at the table, no one seemed to be very hungry any more. No one argued when I offered to take home the leftovers, so I packed them up, then we all pitched in on the check and left. On the drive home I tossed my monstrous packet of forms on the floor of Jason's car, kept my takeout box on my lap, and cranked up the radio, not wanting anymore conversation.

When we pulled up to my house I was relieved to see my mom's car in the driveway. I got out of the car and headed straight for my front door. I waited for Jason to go inside, but he made it obvious that he wanted me to go in first.

Chase waited expectantly, as if he would be coming inside as well. I regarded him. "You're not coming in. Go ahead and call my dad. He can keep you company out here." With that I strode inside and allowed Jason the pleasure of shutting the door in Chase's face.

I quickly forgot my satisfaction as I paused in the living room and took a good look around, completely stunned. The couch, loveseat, and surrounding floor were cluttered with a multitude of shopping bags. Apparently my mom had engaged in a bit of retail therapy. I picked my way through the clutter, then jogged upstairs to her room and went in without knocking. She was passed out on her bed, shoes and trench coat still on.

I let out a sigh of relief, glad that she was home and . . . coping. I tugged off her plain brown shoes and put the royal purple throw from the foot of her bed over her. I closed the door gently as I left her room, even though I doubted anything short of a foghorn could wake her.

I went back downstairs to find Jason standing in the kitchen. His attention was on the window, or more precisely what he could see of Chase through the window. He had resumed his post on my porch swing, gently rocking it back and forth with his feet on the ground. Jason was so intent on trying to make Chase disappear by sheer force of will that I don't think he even heard me approach.

I stepped right in front of him with my arms crossed and cleared my throat loudly.

He looked down at me, brow still furrowed. "I do not like him," he said, referring to Chase.

I shrugged. "Can't say I really blame you."

Jason and I both turned our attention back to the window. As the swing came forward and brought him into full view, Chase gave us a sarcastic salute, making Jason's face turn red with anger. It wasn't like him to lose his temper so easily (that was usually my job), and I wondered if there was something else that had him on edge.

I grabbed his hand and drew him away from the window, then wrapped my arms around his waist in a loose hug. I stared at him until he met my eyes. "Tell me what's wrong," I ordered.

Jason gave me a glimpse of his usual crooked smile. "You are far too perceptive," he conceded.

I smiled back. "Tell me."

"I got a job offer," he said softly.

I cocked my head in question. "So . . . ?"

He licked his lips nervously. "So, I would need to leave immediately."

I broke eye contact and looked down at the floor. "Oh."

"I would not even consider it," he said quickly, then went on more slowly, "but jobs can be few and far between. I can turn down this one, but there is no knowing when the next offer will come along."

"You should take it," I said quickly, knowing that if I took any time to think about it, I'd ask him not to go.

"I know it is bad timing . . . " he began.

"Will you be gone long?" I interrupted, a little more snappishly than I had intended.

"Only a few days," he answered, clearly relieved that I wasn't going to make an extended issue out of him going. "I should be home before Christmas, definitely by your birthday."

My birthday was on the 31st, so that meant he could be gone around 10 days. I nodded despite my feelings. "You leave in the morning?"

He drew me closer, wrapping his arms tightly around me. "Yes," he answered, his lips moving right beside my ear. "I will have to go home to prepare tonight, but I will come by before I leave."

I nodded again and closed my eyes against his shoulder, not sure what else to say. I breathed in the woodsy, vanilla tinted smell of him, not relishing the thought of being away from that scent for even a day.

I felt him glance towards the window again. "If he gives you any trouble, I would like for you to call me immediately."

"I can handle it," I said softly.

"I know," he breathed into my hair.

And just like that, he was gone, shutting the front door silently behind him. I stayed standing in my kitchen for several minutes, my arms wrapped tightly around me. I eventually moved into the living room and tossed my mom's bags onto the floor so I could curl up on the loveseat. I sank into the cushions feeling sorry for myself. I waited, hoping that Jason would come back and reconsider, or that he'd pop in and say, "Gotcha! Just kidding."

When nothing happened, I finally went upstairs to my room. It was close to midnight. I had no idea where the time had gone. I must have sat downstairs for several hours. I walked into my cozy purple-themed bathroom to get ready for bed. I brushed my teeth and scrubbed my face, splashing myself several times with cold water to try and snap myself out of my stupor. I dried myself off with a fluffy purple towel, then forced my eyes up to the mirror.

I looked miserable. I was falling apart because my boyfriend was leaving town during the time I needed him most. It wasn't his fault, but I still felt slightly resentful. Man, I was *pitiful.*

I slapped my hand against the sink with a dull thud, making little sparks of pain run up my wrist. I would *not* fall apart because of a boy. I'd always been able to take care of myself no matter what life threw at me, and damn it, I could handle my situation on my own. I smiled, proud that I had so quickly pulled myself together.

I am demon, hear me roar.

Chapter Eight

There wasn't any fire this time. I was once again on a cold, stone floor, but this time I was lying down with my cheek pressed against the rock. I tried to get up to explore my surroundings, but I couldn't move. I could hear footsteps. Someone came to stand in my field of vision, but all I could see was their shoed feet. The feet kept shifting in shape and color so that I couldn't tell what they looked like. Then the person knelt down beside me, and I knew with sudden certainty that I was going to die.

When I finally woke up the next morning around 9:00, I could vaguely remember Jason coming in through my window in the ungodly early morning hours to say goodbye before he left. My dream had really thrown me. My dreams of fire had always been unnerving, but this one caused me to wake with a solid cold knot of fear in my stomach. I rolled out from underneath my dark green bedspread, hating everything while trying to push my fear aside. I glanced out my large bedroom window to see that the miserable weather matched my mood. Dark grays and blues swirled ominously, promising snow. It was going to be a white Christmas . . . yippee.

I took a shower and got dressed in a deep red cable-knit sweater, and faded, holey jeans shoved into dark brown, low-heeled slouchy boots (courtesy of Allison's annual wardrobe cleansing). Not bothering to do anything with my hair, I clunked downstairs in search of coffee.

I caught sight of my mom sitting at the dining room table dressed in a royal blue sweater dress and black boots. She sipped coffee while carrying on a jovial conversation. My day darkened exponentially when I came around the corner and saw that she was talking to Chase, who looked quite comfortable in his forest green sweater and jeans. He was drinking coffee out of my usual coffee mug. It was oversized and had an illustration of a dejected looking Edgar Allan Poe on one side and was my tried and true favorite.

I walked into the kitchen to find a completely empty coffee pot. I grumbled to myself as I ground some beans and got a fresh pot going. I grabbed a store-bought blueberry muffin and stomped back into the dining room, taking a seat on the far side of the table, away from my mom and Chase. They interrupted their conversation to turn their attention to me.

I regarded my mom, ignoring Chase's presence. "No work today?"

"No," she answered, a big, fake smile plastered across her face. "I'm feeling kinda tired," she went on, her smile crumbling around the edges.

I nodded, understanding that she still wasn't ready to discuss things further. She gave me a genuine, if small, smile in return.

"So," my mom began awkwardly, "I found your friend on the porch and invited him in to wait for you." She smiled warmly at Chase, but I could sense her wariness underneath.

My smile for Chase was more of a snarl. "He's not my friend," I corrected, making eye contact with Chase as I said it.

"Oh," my mom hesitated. "Well, um, I have a lot of gift wrapping to do, so I'll leave you two alone." She stood and hustled out of the dining room. I caught her glancing back into the dining room with motherly concern before she turned to hurry up the stairs. I had a feeling the days of my mom prying were at an end. She could never be sure what information she might pry her way into.

I turned my attention to Chase. "You got a car?"

He smiled pleasantly at me despite my earlier rudeness. "I can get one," he answered simply.

I nodded and stood to get myself a cup of coffee. Chase stood as well and immediately let himself out the front door, presumably to "get" a car. I hadn't felt the need to let him in on the fact that I just wanted him to take me to the mall to finish my Christmas shopping; he might not have deemed it important enough.

I sat back down at the table with hot coffee and my muffin and couldn't help my mischievous grin. Messing with Chase had made me feel infinitely better. I would have to continue doing so. My thoughts went to Jason, and I immediately redirected them. What else did I need to buy for Christmas . . . oh who was I kidding? I stared down into my coffee cup and wallowed.

By the time Chase returned, I had finished my coffee and muffin and was leafing through a catalogue while I waited. I grabbed my keys and wallet to throw into a plain cloth purse I had recently bought and went outside to meet him. The cloudy sky had made me expect miserably weather, but the air felt cool and calm. I still expected snow, but maybe it would be the pleasant, soft-falling snow that's so popular in Hallmark commercials, rather than the harsh, blizzardy snow that was more often the reality.

Chase was leaning against an ancient gray, rust-speckled pickup truck. I had serious doubts that it would even make it to the mall. He stepped away from the truck and swung his arms out to pose like a model on a game show. "Your chariot awaits," he said dramatically.

I raised my eyebrows. "Lovely," I replied sarcastically.

Chase smiled and went around to get in the driver's side. I yanked the passenger door open and climbed into the ancient seat. Chase shut his door and started the ignition. I squirmed as I tried to find a position where the seat springs wouldn't poke into me through the seat's flattened padding. I finally settled in with a disgruntled expression.

Chase, misreading my expression of distaste asked, "Did you want to drive or something?"

I paused a moment in confusion, then seeing an opportunity, quickly hoisted my nose into the air, as if offended that he had assumed the role of driver without asking me. "Yes, yes I do."

He didn't even argue. He just got out and went around to the passenger's side while I slid into the driver's seat. I couldn't help but be pleased. My driving terrifies my mom, so since I don't have a car of my own, I didn't get to drive often. I was practically bouncing up and down with excitement by the time Chase finished buckling himself into the passenger's seat.

Taking in my maniacal glee, he looked at me nervously. "Something tells me I'm going to regret this."

I took the time to flash him a quick grin, then slammed my foot on the gas.

The truck peeled out of my driveway, kicking gravel up in its wake. The old clunker had a lot more power than my mom's little car. I eased off the gas just a little bit as we wove through my neighborhood towards the highway.

I spared a quick glance at Chase. "Mind if we take the long way?"

"Sure," he said weakly.

I drove a short way on the small highway that leads through the middle of town, then turned onto a street that would take me to the back roads. I was mainly going this way to avoid the graveyard, but I'd let Chase believe that I just wanted a chance to drive the truck on the long, curvy back roads. Heck, he'd be partially right to believe so.

As soon as we reached the start of the narrow road that curves out into the woods on the outskirts of Shelby, I let my foot fall down on the gas. Chase was beginning to look a bit more relaxed, so I rolled down my window and hit the gas a little bit more. The wind blowing in through the window pummeled me, making my hair swirl around my head. Since I hadn't done anything to my hair that morning anyways, I wasn't about to worry about it.

Chase cranked up the ancient radio, then started flipping through the few stations that we get in Shelby. He settled on a station that was playing *Living on a Thin Line* by the Kinks, then leaned back against his seat.

As we made our way down the deserted road, partially shaded by the surrounding trees, I eased my foot off the gas a bit. For the first time in days, a feeling of relaxed contentment came over me. Chase may not have been my first choice for company, but the wind in my hair felt good, and we were in little danger of being attacked or confronted by anyone or anything. My thoughts wandered to Jason, and the fact that I didn't even know where he was going or what his "job" was. I quickly stifled the irritation that bubbled in me, not wanting to ruin the peacefulness of the moment.

Thinking it was as good a time as any, I turned down the radio and rolled my window up partially so I could talk to Chase. I waited in the relative silence for him to turn his attention from the window to me. When he didn't I cleared my throat.

He turned to me, startled out of his thoughts.

Keeping my attention on the road, I asked, "Now that we're alone, are you ready to explain to me just how you know my dad, and why he chose you to 'protect' me?"

He was silent for a moment, then answered softly, "I owe your dad a favor, really, I owe him my life."

I raised my eyebrows at that, and spared Chase a quick glance to assure myself that he wasn't messing with me. "Seriously?"

"Yeah."

"And . . . ?"

He cleared his throat. "And . . . that's it."

I let that line of conversation drop, not that I was done with it, but I could stand to postpone it until he was feeling slightly more sharing. "So . . . " I began, "Jason said that you smell like me, like a demon."

"Yes," he replied, not elaborating any further.

I pinched my lips in frustration. "What gives? You said you would explain things to me once we were alone."

He sighed loudly. "Yes, I'm a demon too. My mom was a full demon, and my dad was a half demon."

"So you're more demon-y than I am?" I interrupted.

He smiled. "In an inconsequential kind of way. Demons have different bloodlines; the more powerful the bloodline, the more powerful the demon. The more powerful the demon, the more traits they will pass on to their offspring. Your dad comes from a very powerful bloodline. My parents were both from mixed bloodlines."

"So . . ." I prompted.

"So," he went on, "though I have more demon blood than you, you're slightly more 'demon-y' than me."

"How demon-y are you?" I pressed. "What can you do?"

He resigned himself to our line of conversation and began to explain, "I'm told that my dad was a necro-demon, he could speak to the dead and create zombies, and my mom was half-Nāga."

I pursed my lips in stunned thought for a minute. And here I was thinking that nothing could shock me anymore. "Okay, first, necro-demon? And second, what the heck is a Nāga? And why do you say 'I'm told'?"

He smiled bitterly. "First, yes, necro-demon. Second, a Nāga in the most simple terms is a snake person. Third, I say 'I'm told' because my parents abandoned me when I was young." He said everything as if it was very matter-of-fact, with no emotion whatsoever.

I decided that I probably didn't know him well enough to question him further about being abandoned. It could be a sore subject. I should know. "So what can you do?"

He seemed relieved that I had taken my questioning in this direction. "Well," he began, "working with the dead is mostly beyond me. I can see ghosts and spirits, and sometimes talk to them, but that's about it. I have the regular demon traits: extra strength, sharpened senses, better healing. I'm probably stronger in those areas than you, just because of the amount of demon blood I have. It's the actual powers I'm more lacking in. Also, from my mom's side, I'm slightly poisonous."

Oh ick. "In what way?" I asked.

He turned to me and grinned, showing teeth. Two tiny fangs appeared at his gum line and slowly extended over his canines. I almost swerved off the road watching them.

He laughed then looked back out the windshield. "In that way," he answered.

"Oh," I replied, feeling a major case of heebie-jeebies. Enough of that subject. "And why do you owe my dad your life?"

He cringed, then glanced at me nervously. "Another time?" he asked.

"Sure," I conceded, "another time."

He slumped down in his seat, as if giving me all this information had cost him a great deal. Who knew? Maybe it had.

By the time we finally pulled up to the mall, I had gone into full relaxation mode. I know it was a bit odd, that I was only able to finally relax in the presence of a stranger, one who I should have known better than to be relaxed around, but there it was regardless. It was nice to be away from responsibilities and expectations.

I manually rolled up the window, and Chase and I both stepped out of the rickety truck. I had to slam my door twice to get it to latch, then we both headed towards the mall. Chase walked casually by my side, holding the door open for me with a slightly mocking smile. I walked through nonchalantly, not bothering to catch the door on the interior to hold it open for him. I was instantly bombarded by the chaos of a shopping center a week before Christmas. I sent a brief angry thought to my dad, blaming him for the fact that I had to come to the mall twice in one week.

The only person I had left to buy for was Jason, and I was still at a loss as to what to get him. I figured Barnes & Noble was as good a place to start as any, and made a beeline for the store with Chase hot on my heels. Once in the store, I began browsing the shelves with the idea that I could simply buy him a bunch of books, and hopefully equal, but not outdo whatever he got for me.

Chase leaned in over my shoulder, his face uncomfortably close to mine. His shampoo smelled like oranges. "Who ya shopping for?" he asked in a sing-song manner.

I sidestepped to put some space between us. "None of your business," I grumbled.

Chase made a hmmf sound in his throat, then held up a finger, as if experiencing an epiphany. "Aaah, shopping for the vampire, are we?"

I glared at him. "Yes, if you must know. My dad interrupted my shopping the other day. Jason's was the only gift I didn't get."

Chase simply nodded and strolled away to a different shelf of books, hands clasped behind his back casually. My relaxed ease officially crushed, I turned my attention back to my task. I was beginning to think that the bookstore was a lost cause, because I couldn't be sure what Jason had or hadn't read. Then my eyes were drawn to a collection on an end-cap. I walked closer to investigate, realizing that the collection was a boxed set of fifteen classics. Bingo. I swiped up the box, not bothering to check the price, and headed to the register.

After I payed, I started looking around for Chase, who was nowhere to be seen. I deduced that he wasn't anywhere in the store, so I walked out into the crowded concourse to look for him. The place was a madhouse, and I resigned myself to the possibility that it could be awhile before I found him, and I had stupidly handed him the truck keys. Not that I would strand him at the mall. No . . . neeever.

Just as I was about to park my butt on a bench to wait, Chase came striding towards me with a coffee cup in each hand. As he approached he extended one out to me. "Peace offering?" he said with a smile.

I switched my shopping bag to my left hand and took the offered coffee with a glare. "You make it very hard to dislike you."

Chase's smile grew as he rocked back and forth on his heels. "Then I suggest you stop trying."

I smirked at him, then turned to walk back towards the closest exit.

Chase caught up to walk shoulder to shoulder with me. "You done already?"

I nodded. The exit was in sight. Eye on the prize, eye on the prize. I'd be away from the bustling crowd soon.

"Did you get anything for your dad?"

I stopped and spun on Chase. "Are you kidding?"

Chase raised his dark eyebrows at my reaction. "Why would I be kidding? He *has* afforded you your very own bodyguard," he said, putting his arms out and looking himself up and down.

I let out a harsh breath. "And that's supposed to make up for not being around my entire life?"

"No," Chase said apathetically, "but it's a start."

I just stared at him, at a loss for words.

He made a calming gesture with his free hand. "Sorry, sorry. I concede to your point. Now drink your coffee."

I took a sip, more to cover up how flustered I was than anything. Creamy deliciousness poured down my throat. Delighted, I asked, "What on earth is this wonderful concoction?"

"Breve," Chase responded, laughing at me. "It's like a latte, but they use half-and-half instead of milk."

I smiled. "You are fully forgiven. Let's go." We went.

Chapter Nine

It was already 3:00 pm when we got back to my house. My mom's car was missing from the driveway again. I went inside, grudgingly inviting Chase in with me, and learned from my mom's note that she was indulging in more retail therapy. She had probably been at the mall when we were, but it was so crowded I wasn't surprised we hadn't run into her.

I walked to the machine and pushed the button below the flashing red light. The first message was from one of my mom's coworkers and I skipped over it after a few seconds. Lucy's voice played out of the machine next. "Xoe, it's Lucy. We can't find Lela. She was supposed to meet me and Max hours ago. Call me back."

Lucy's message clicked off and I jumped when my dad's voice began to play. "Alexondra, stay near Chase. We need to talk." Click. Ominous, very ominous.

I turned towards Chase, who had been listening over my shoulder. "Any idea what he wants?"

Chase shrugged. "Not a clue. Lela was one of the werewolves we met at the pizza parlor, right?"

I nodded as a sick feeling sunk into my gut. Something was very wrong. My skin started to prickle with an electric sensation. A moment later, there was a knock on the door.

"It's your dad." Chase stated.

I went to answer the door, figuring the prickle had been me sensing my dad's peculiar form of teleportation. Maybe I could learn that one too. Now that would be nice.

As soon as I opened the door, my dad came striding in, looking expensive in black slacks and a dark blue cashmere sweater. "A witch was abducted in Bear Creek," he stated, anger tinting his words. Bear Creek was another small town within an hour of Shelby.

"They're getting closer," Chase observed.

"Well duh," I added. Then turning toward my dad I asked, "I take it we should be worried?"

He nodded, making his blond hair fall forward from behind his ears. "I will protect you," he said.

"I don't want your protection," I replied sullenly.

"But you need it anyhow."

I barely heard my dad's last statement. A horrible idea had dawned on me. "Lela's missing."

My dad looked at me, obvious surprise showing on his face. "One of your wolves?"

I nodded.

My dad nodded somberly. "They're here then."

My palms began to sweat from my nerves. I suddenly didn't feel safe at all. "What do we do?"

Chase put a hand on my shoulder. "No one's going to take you."

I shrugged his hand off and turned to face him. "That's not what I was asking!" I shouted. "How do we find Lela?"

"Calm down Alexondra," my dad said flatly. "You will stay here with Chase. I will find your wolf."

Before I could argue, my dad strode straight out the front door, closing it behind him. I ran to the door and flung it open, but all that was left was a wisp of smoke and a scorch mark on the gravel. Unable to argue with my dad, I slammed the door shut and stomped to the phone. I picked it up and quickly dialed Lucy's number.

She picked up on the first ring. "Xoe?" Lucy's voice questioned.

"We think Lela was taken," I said quickly. "You and Max should come to my house."

"Safety in numbers?" Lucy questioned.

"Something like that," I muttered.

"I'll call Max. See you soon." She hung up.

Feeling numb, I gently set the phone back in the cradle. Chase was watching me from across the room, still standing where I left him. "We can't go looking for her," he said, referring to Lela.

I shook my head in frustration. "Who said I was going to look for her?"

Chase raised a sarcastic eyebrow at me, but said nothing.

"Okay, okay." I raised my hands in submission. "So the thought had crossed my mind, but I have no clue where to start looking."

Chase sighed loudly. "Where was she seen last?"

I smiled. "So you'll help?"

He grimaced, then nodded slowly. "Just don't make me regret it."

My smile grew. "We have to wait for Lucy and Max. They'll know where she was."

Chase nodded. "We'll all go there together. I doubt we'll find any clues, but in the very least Max and Lucy might find a scent."

I nodded, feeling relieved to at least have a semblance of a plan. "Sounds good." Then after a horribly loud growl from my stomach, I added, "You hungry?"

Chase finally smiled, if a little weakly. "Starved."

I went into the kitchen to rummage. Chase came into the kitchen as I was pawing through the few items in our fridge. I took out a cardboard carton of Chinese food and opened it to take a whiff. Satisfied, I handed the carton to Chase and reached in for the others. We zapped them all in the microwave. Then with forks in hand, went to the dining room table.

We sat, and I grabbed the box of Mongolian beef right before Chase could snatch it for himself. He frowned, then went for the sweet-and-sour chicken. I took my first bite of food and smiled smugly at him.

"So," I began around a mouthful of broccoli, "do we have any idea what type of, um, creatures are behind the abductions?"

Chase shook his head, not looking up from his food. "Obviously someone, or something pretty strong, seeing as they were able to abduct witches and werewolves."

"And merpeople," I added.

"Yeah, but merpeople aren't any stronger that regular humans. They just swim faster."

I nodded. "Learn something new every day."

There was a knock at the door. Chase set down his box of chicken to get up and answer it. I heard the door open, then Lucy's voice as her and Max came in.

Lucy entered the dining room first, looking disheveled in blue plaid flannel and jeans, with her hair a staticy mess around her delicate face. She took the chair across from me that Chase had used and slumped down in the seat as if exhausted. She eyed the boxes of Chinese food skeptically, then at my arched eyebrow, started filling me in on the details. "We were all supposed to meet at Max's house," she began. "We knew Lela had a job interview this morning, so we didn't worry at first when she was late. But then an hour went by, and we still hadn't heard from her. I called her cell phone and a stranger answered. He said he had just found her phone lying in the middle of the sidewalk."

Chase pulled out the chair beside Lucy, while Max took the seat to my left. Max was dressed in a bright yellow sweater and his usual khaki cargo pants.

Chase turned to Lucy. "Did he say where he was when he found it?"

Lucy nodded. "The phone was outside of Blue Moon coffee shop. He told us he'd leave it inside with the cashier. Blue Moon is right across the street from the bank where Lela was supposed to interview."

I pushed away my unfinished Mongolian beef. "Well I guess that's where we'll start."

"What about that other guy?" Chase asked.

"Nick?" Lucy responded. "We haven't seen him since yesterday. We don't even know how to get a hold of him."

I sighed. "Great, just great."

We all stood to leave, abandoning the leftover Chinese on the table. I grabbed my cloth purse and shiny dark brown leather jacket as we walked out the door. Chase locked and shut the door behind us, then fished in his pocket for the truck keys, which he then tossed to me. I caught them one-handed, then noticed the box of Chinese food in his hand. It was my discarded Mongolian beef.

Noticing my glance, he produced a fork from his back pocket. He put a bite of beef and broccoli in his mouth and chewed slowly with a pleased smile on his face. I laughed despite our dire situation. I just couldn't help it.

We all piled into the ancient truck, Lucy squished into the middle of the front seat between Chase and me, while Max squeezed into one of those pointless little fold-down seats that some pick-up trucks have behind the front seat.

"Whose truck is this?" Lucy asked as we pulled out of the driveway on onto the street.

"Chase's," I answered.

Chase cleared his throat. "Technically, it's Xoe's dad's truck. He bought it."

I turned towards him, almost swerving off the road. "So when you left, you had my dad buy you a truck?"

Chase had the courtesy to look abashed. "No. I bought it, but I bought it with the expense account your dad allowed me while I'm watching you."

Watching me? It seriously chaffed to have to take so much help from my dad, but I would not pout. When life hands you demons . . . well, you get the idea.

Chase was still waiting for my reaction. I put a pleasant smile on my face. "Well, now that I know that, I know who'll be paying for stuff from now on."

Chase smiled back mischievously and produced a wallet from his pocket, then picked out a blue credit card to hold up. "You've got yourself a deal."

As I exited onto the highway, I glanced at Max in the rearview mirror. A look of astonishment was plastered on his face. Lucy looked like she had eaten something sour. I realized that a lot had changed between Chase and me in the course of one day. It was nice to have a companion that didn't ask anything of me, except that he had to stay by my side. My thoughts fluttered to Jason, wondering where he was and what he was doing. I was going to have to make a phone call and get some answers.

We were nearing the exit that would take us to what I thought of as the pedestrian area of Shelby. The few roads that the area consisted of were populated with a few coffee shops, bookstores, bars, restaurants, and some random curio shops. There was one large parking lot, and the few other spots were all parallel parking, so most people parked in the lot and walked to their destination.

I took the exit, then only had to drive another minute or so to reach the lot. I took the first available spot next to several motorcycles. We all got out and began to walk the three street blocks to Blue Moon. Though it was only around 5:00 pm, it was also December in Oregon, so the sun was slowly making its descent behind the mountains. There weren't many people out. Most of the coffee shop goers had gone home, and the bar and restaurant goers were yet to surface.

First we visited the bank where Lela was supposed to interview, but it had just closed, so we went across the street to the coffee shop, which was open until 9:00. Blue moon is one of the fancier coffee shops in Shelby, but they scoff at any request for a $1.50 regular coffee, so I almost never go there.

As we entered the glass double-doors, I was instantly soothed by the warm ambiance and the scent of vanilla and coffee. The upper walls and ceiling were done in a midnight blue, with tiny pinpricks of fiber-optic light scattered everywhere, and the lower walls were an opalescent white. Blue Moon may be overpriced, but you sure have to hand it to them on the décor.

I walked up to the dark blue countertop to order a cup of coffee and ask some questions. Lucy and Max sat at a table by the window, while Chase came to stand beside me at the counter. A tall young woman with tightly curled red hair, fair, freckled skin, and pale green eyes approached the register. She wore a black polo and a black apron with moons and stars on it that was standard issue for the Blue Moon staff. Her nametag said "Megan". I didn't recognize her as anyone I'd seen working there before, though like I said, I didn't go there often.

She smiled a little too pleasantly at me, revealing perfectly straight white teeth. "What can I get for you?" she asked in an overly perky voice.

I couldn't remember the name of what Chase had gotten us at the mall, so I turned to him to order. Chase looked down at me with an awkward wideness to his eyes, like he was trying to tell me something. He turned back to the woman and gave her a charming smile. "Four tall breves please."

"Will that be all?" the woman asked in a sing-song voice.

"Yes it will," I answered. "By the way, are you new here? I haven't seen you around."

The woman's smile faltered around the edges. "Yes, yes I am."

I was about to ask about Lela's cell phone, but Chase kicked my foot in warning. I gave him a dirty look, but didn't argue as he handed the woman his card to pay for our coffees. I left him at the counter to sign the receipt and joined Max and Lucy at the table.

Chase waited at the counter while the woman made our coffees, then made two short trips to carry them to our table before he sat beside me. After he placed the second set of coffees on the table, he leaned over to me and put his lips by my ear in a strangely intimate gesture. I started to pull away, but then realized that he was trying to tell me something. "She's not human," he breathed.

I pulled away and giggled as if he had said something horribly amusing. I leaned towards his ear flirtatiously and whispered, "What is she?"

He put his arm around me and pulled my ear close to him again. "I don't know," he whispered. "Max or Lucy might be able to tell if they've encountered the scent before."

Max and Lucy had been pretending to ignore us, but with their werewolf hearing, they had probably heard every word. Max confirmed my suspicions when he stood and walked up to the cashier. He came back after a few seconds with a little shaker full of cinnamon. Max gave the barest shrug as he sat back down. He hadn't recognized the scent, which meant she wasn't werewolf, vampire, or demon.

Lucy caught my eyes, then glanced back at the counter. The woman had been watching us throughout our exchange. She quickly turned around to busy herself at the espresso machine as soon as I looked at her. I glanced back to my companions, who all nodded. We stood with our coffees and left the coffee shop. As the doors swung shut behind us, I stole a final glance inside. The woman was typing something on a cell phone.

The sky had almost darkened completely now. There was no moon, making that darkness even more ominous above the streetlights. I huddled in my jacket, suddenly feeling even colder than the weather could make me. Chase hustled us all forward. "We need to go," he said quietly.

I felt eyes on me. I glanced across the street to see a pale-skinned man with a buzz-cut, dressed in a dark colored suit. He stood watching us from a corner almost out of reach of the nearest streetlight. I suppressed a shudder. 'You don't have to tell me twice," I mumbled as we cut around a street corner towards the parking lot.

I came to a skidding halt as soon as we went around the corner, right as we came face to face with none other than my friendly neighbor Brian. I quickly managed to close my gaping jaw and recover. Then I proceeded to brush by him without giving him a single extra glance of recognition.

"Seriously Xoe?" he called from behind us.

I paused long enough to turn and face him. "Sorry, didn't know if talking to you might be too *weird*." I held up my arms to gesture to the streets around us. "And we're obviously not behind closed doors."

Taking a great deal of satisfaction in Brian's stunned expression, I turned back around and we continued walking as if nothing had happened. Well I acted as if nothing had happened. Lucy and Max were grinning from ear-to-ear. I wished I could smile too, but I had just caught sight of crew-cut man across the street.

We walked un-accosted the rest of the way to the truck. I handed Chase the keys, feeling too shaken to drive. We all piled in and let out a shared breath as the truck started and we pulled out of the lot. Lucy had opted for the other pull down seat in the back rather than squeezing in the middle of the front again.

"Do you see anyone?" Chase asked.

We all looked out the windows as we pulled onto the street that would lead us back to the highway. The early bar crowd was beginning to pour in, but no one seemed to pay us any mind. "I don't know," I answered. "Did you notice the guy on the street corner? I think he followed us down the block."

Chase nodded. Lucy and Max remained silent. My shoulders eased as we merged onto the highway. Max popped his head up amongst us in the front seat. "I didn't recognize the smell. She smelled like ozone and blood."

"Blood?" Lucy asked nervously.

"Yeah," Max went on, "and something else I couldn't quite place, kinda like cinnamon or something."

"What do we do now?" I asked.

Chase spared me a quick glance. "We should call your dad, at least let him know what we've found."

I nodded to myself. "Okay, we'll let him know. But after that, what do we do?"

We were nearing the exit to my neighborhood. Chase was silent. He glanced at the rearview mirror, then sped right past the exit.

"Umm . . . " I began.

Chase sped up. "Someone's following us."

I turned to look out the back windshield as Lucy and Max did the same. We were on the highway, and even though Shelby's highway is relatively small, there were still several cars in the lanes behind us. "Which one?" I asked.

Chase glanced in the mirror. "Dark blue minivan."

I turned back towards Chase. "Seriously? We're being followed by a *minivan*?"

Chase nodded, then took the exit that would lead us to the abandoned industrial district. I hated the industrial district. It was the place where Lucy had first turned into a werewolf. I hated it almost as much as I hated the graveyard . . . almost. The minivan exited right behind us.

We reached the two-lane road of the industrial district and began to speed down the dilapidated road. I had a brief moment to wonder why of all exits Chase would pick the traffic-less industrial district, then the truck was spinning in a tight u-turn. The tires came to a screeching halt. A few seconds later the minivan sped right past us. They were going so fast they would have hit us had we simply decided to brake in front of them. Before the minivan could manage to slow enough to turn around, Chase sped back down the road and onto the exit ramp, going the wrong way.

"What are you doing!" I screamed, frantically holding on to the sides of my seat.

Chase ignored me, his full attention focused on the road. He picked up even more speed as we approached the highway and oncoming traffic. I cursed silently to myself. We were going to die. The minivan had caught back up, and was following close behind us.

Chase shot out onto the highway, right in front of a red sports car whose driver held down on his horn until we cleared that side of the highway. Chase eased the truck into traffic, heading back the way we had just come.

I slowly unclenched my fingers from the seat cushion, and turned to look back at Max and Lucy. Their faces had drained of color, and both held identical, horror-stricken expressions. I turned my attention back to Chase, who was looking out the rear-view mirror with a tense squint to his eyes.

"Are you completely insane?" I asked.

He didn't answer right away. I stole a quick glance behind us. The minivan was nowhere in sight. Chase nodded to himself, satisfied. "I think we lost them."

I snorted in disbelief. "Yeah, and we almost lost our lives too."

Chase ignored my comment. "My guess is that we just had a close brush with the infamous abductors."

"Why were they following us?" I asked.

Chase glanced at me before taking an exit that would lead us to the larger part of Shelby where Irvine's pizza was. "Well, they've abducted witches, werewolves, and merpeople, so it's safe to say they have a way of identifying supernaturals. They've been picking them off one by one. Now they've found four of us together."

"Where are we going?" Lucy chimed in.

Chase took a left turn, then sped up and took a quick right. "I want to make sure no one's following us before we go back to Xoe's."

"What do we do then?" I asked.

Chase took another left, leading us farther away from the highway. "We call your dad."

"And?" I pressed.

Chase pursed his lips in frustration. "And that's it," he answered. "I've put you in enough danger already. We shouldn't have come."

"We had to come," I countered. "They have Lela. Who knows what they're doing to her? We don't even know if she's still alive."

A chill went down my spine. There was a very real possibility that Lela was dead. I should have listened to my dad. We should have made a plan to stick together as soon as we found out about the abductions.

"We should go back to the coffee shop," I suggested. "We can wait until that girl leaves, then we can follow her."

Chase sighed, then lifted off the seat to dig in his pants' pocket. He pulled out a slim black cell phone and handed it to me. "Call your dad. His number's in the contacts list."

I stared at the cell phone for a minute before flipping it open. Lucy and Max were completely silent in the backseat. *Alexandre* was the first name on the short list of contacts. I selected his name and pushed the call button before I had a chance to think better of it.

He picked up on the first ring. "Where are you? I've been trying to find you, but you keep moving."

"What?" I asked, confused. "How'd you know we were moving?"

"Alexondra?" he inquired. Then before I could answer he went on, "You were supposed to stay home. Where are you?"

"We're driving," I snapped. "We found the abductors at Blue Moon coffee shop. We're going back to follow them."

"Absolutely not," he snapped back. "Where is Chase? Let me talk to him."

I extended the phone out to Chase, who took it while glaring at me. We were reaching the end of town and entering a wealthy residential area. The manicured lawns and white picket fences seemed sorely out of place with what was going on.

"Would you rather I had let her go alone?" Chase argued with the phone. He paused to listen, then nodded to himself. "We have the other two wolves with us." He listened to the phone for another minute then handed it back to me.

"What?" I asked after I pushed the phone against my ear.

My dad grunted at my rudeness. "You will all be returning to your home now. I'm going to the coffee shop."

"Then we'll meet you there," I argued.

"No," was his only reply.

"We can help!" I practically shouted.

"Think Alexondra," he replied calmly. "They know what you look like. They haven't seen me yet. I will be able to follow them."

I let out a frustrated breath. He was right, and oh how it rankled. "Fine," I grumbled. "And don't call me Alexondra," I added, but he had already hung up.

Chase had navigated his way through the residential area, only to end up at the mall. I gave a confused look as we entered the mall parking lot. I had never known about this round-about way to get to the mall. He shrugged at my look. Apparently he hadn't known either.

"Why are we going to the mall?" Max asked, startling me. I had forgotten that Lucy and him were back there.

"We're not," Chase answered. "We're going to take the back way to Xoe's. I don't want to risk being seen on the highway."

We drove straight through the mall parking lot and out the back exit that led to the forest road we had taken before. A question I had came back to me. "How was my dad planning to find us? How did he know that we were moving?"

Chase shrugged. "It's a demon thing. We can sense each other."

"Could you find me like that?" I asked.

"Probably," he answered. "It gets easier to sense you the longer I know you, only when you're awake though. It has something to do with the brainwaves."

Now *that* was creepy. I didn't think I liked the idea of my dad and Chase being able to find me wherever I went, though I guess I didn't really have a choice.

Lucy leaned forward to rest her chin on the back of the front seat. "Could you find one of us?" she asked. "Someone who isn't part demon?"

I knew she was thinking about Lela. Chase shook his head apologetically. "No."

I couldn't believe how calmly we were conversing. I couldn't believe how calm I felt, how unafraid. My once normal friends and I had adapted to a completely new life, a life where kidnappings and high-speed chases were nothing to get too worked up about. Heck, even Allison had adapted, and she was human.

I turned to share a knowing look with Lucy. Just call us Electra Woman and Dyna Girl.

Chapter Ten

It was full dark by the time we reached my house, and my dad still hadn't called. I noticed that my mom's car had returned to its normal spot as we parked in my driveway. We walked inside my dimly lit house to the sound of Christmas music.

I stifled a groan when I realized that the dim lighting was candlelight, with our colorfully decorated artificial tree as the brightly lit centerpiece. The smell of baked goods was in the air, and I knew something was wrong right there. My mom almost never baked. The last time she had baked was the morning after the Dan conflict. I had broken my arm and my mom was forced to come home from a business trip in Washington to bail me out of the hospital.

My mom came out of the kitchen in a red and green apron with matching pot-holders, a pan of chocolate chip cookies grasped between her protected hands. "Cookies?" she offered, her smile a little too wide. It had to be overwhelming for her, being confronted by my friends and me now that she knew what we were. Well, she didn't know what Chase was, but I'm sure she had her suspicions.

I forced myself to smile. "Um, sure."

My mom took that as answer enough and turned to go back into the kitchen. Lucy and I followed her in while Chase and Max went to sit in the living room. My mom set the pan of cookies onto the stove, then looked startled when she turned around to see Lucy and me behind her.

My mom pulled a spatula out of the cylinder that holds our cooking utensils and began lifting the cookies onto a large red plate. "Does everyone want milk?" she asked. "I made cinnamon rolls too. Oh, and we could have coffee . . . "

"Okay mom," I interrupted. "Why don't you let Lucy and me handle this? You can go talk to Max and Chase."

She nodded. "Oh, okay." She nodded again to herself and exited the kitchen.

Lucy's eyes followed her out with a worried cast to them. Lucy turned her almond shaped brown eyes back to me. "Your mom is acting really weird . . . and where's Jason?"

"She knows everything," I began. I ignored Lucy's gaping jaw and went on, "and Jason has a job. He had to leave town."

"Wait, what?" Lucy stuttered. "You told her? And how could Jason leave? We need him here." She pointed her finger dramatically at the ground.

I started shoveling the rest of the cookies onto the plate, but then paused to go to the adjacent counter and start a pot of coffee. Lucy followed right behind me, still waiting for an explanation. I gave her a tired expression as I poured beans into the coffee grinder. "He had to go. Who knows when another job will come along? He has to take what he can get."

Lucy put a hand on her hip and looked at me skeptically. "It doesn't sound like you really believe that."

I shook my head. "I believe it. I know he had to go, but it doesn't make me feel any better about it."

"Have you called him to let him know what's going on?" she asked.

I shook my head.

"Xoe!" she exclaimed. She cringed and lowered her voice. "You need to call him. He's going to be furious when he finds out that you were in danger and didn't tell him."

"I know," I conceded as I filled the pot with water and pressed the start button. "But I can take care of myself."

"And you wouldn't mind making him a little furious?" Lucy added.

I thought about it for a moment. I was pissed that he left right after my dad came into town. I had to admit, the idea of making Jason angry was rather appealing. I laughed a harsh sound that didn't really sound like a laugh at all. "Yeah, that too."

Lucy shook her head in exasperation, but let the subject drop. "What exactly did you tell your mom?"

I went back to shoveling cookies, and Lucy once again followed me. "Pretty much everything," I answered. "Except for what happened with Dan."

Lucy shooed me to the side so she could open the oven and pull out the cinnamon rolls with one of my

121

mom's oven mitts. She placed them onto the now empty cookie pan. I searched the cabinets until I found a large plastic platter to put them on. As Lucy lifted the cinnamon rolls off the pan, I got out mugs for everyone to have coffee or milk.

Lucy stopped me before I headed into the living room with the mugs. "Is that why she's baking?" she whispered.

I nodded. "She likes to be occupied when she's trying to cope with something."

I grabbed a stack of paper plates to put under my arm, then took the mugs into the living room and handed them out, leaving the last two on the coffee table for Lucy and me. Chase and Max were on the large blue sofa, looking uncomfortable as my mom made conversation with them from her perch on the smaller green loveseat. Lucy followed me out with the tray of cookies and a jug of milk. I handed my mom the plates, then set the tray on the coffee table for Lucy. I went back to the kitchen alone for the cinnamon rolls and coffee.

I re-entered the living room and squeezed the cinnamon rolls onto the coffee table beside the cookies, but had to settle with leaving the coffee pot on our single end table. Everyone had already filled their mugs with milk, leaving me with the entire pot of coffee to myself. I was on a bit of a coffee overload already, but hey, it helped me cope. Some people bake, some people drink coffee.

Lucy had taken the seat by my mom, so I sat next to Max on the couch. My mom smiled at all of us, some of her usual warmth creeping through. "Where's Allison?" she asked.

I turned to Lucy. "Where *is* Allison?"

Lucy cocked her head as she reached for a cinnamon roll to put on the plate my mom had handed her. "You know what? I haven't heard from her all day."

"I'll call her," Max added, anticipating our worry. Plus, he was always willing to call Allison. I sensed a crush, but he never openly admitted it. He stood up to go to the phone and I busied myself with piling several cookies and a cinnamon roll onto my plate. Max took the phone into the kitchen.

My mom turned her attention to Lucy. "So you're a werewolf then?"

Lucy choked on her bite of cinnamon roll, then took a big gulp of milk to wash it down. She set her plate in her lap and nervously brushed a strand of her straight dark hair behind her ear. "Um . . . yeah, yes I am."

My mom smiled again, looking almost demented with nerves. "And Max too?"

Max came back into the room with the phone and distractedly answered my mom. "Yeah, I am too." He turned his gaze to me. "Allison went with Lela to her job interview."

My mom turned to me. "Lela? Is that the woman who was here before?"

I nodded in response and began to stand. My mom mirrored me, but then Chase came to the rescue and asked her about her work, forcing her to remain in the living room out of politeness. I grabbed Max and dragged him back into the kitchen.

"She never came home?" I prodded in a hoarse whisper. My heart was racing with adrenaline. I already knew the answer.

Max shook his head. "No. Her parents aren't worried yet. They figure she's still just hanging out with Lela. I didn't tell them any different, but I imagine they'll call the cops if she's not home within the next few hours."

I clenched back the first of my tears. "What are we going to do?" I breathed.

Max's pale green eyes glistened with unshed tears as well. It was like Allison was already dead. Please don't let her be dead.

"What about the coalition?" Max whispered.

"Even if they could get here in time, I don't even know how to get a hold of them."

"Where's Jason?" He asked, as if just realizing what was missing from the situation. I couldn't blame him, we hadn't had much time to stop and think lately.

"He's on a job," I answered dejectedly as a cursed tear slipped out.

"Everything all right in there?" my mom called.

"Fine mom!" I yelled back.

I heard Chase's voice rise with his next question to distract my mom again.

Max waved his hand in my face to bring my attention back to him. "Call him," he demanded.

"But," I argued. "It's not going to do any good."

"Call him," Max intoned again, this time slapping the portable phone into my palm.

With a quivering sigh, I turned my back on Max and punched in the cell phone numbers I knew by heart.

He picked up on the second ring. "Xoe?"

"Yeah," I breathed. "It's me."

"What is wrong?" he asked. "Something is wrong. I can hear it in your voice."

"Lela and Allison are both missing," I answered. "We're pretty positive they've been abducted."

"I am coming home," he said gravely, not missing a beat. "I'm in New York. It's going to take me a day or so to get there."

"It's okay," I answered, tears flowing freely. "We just need Abel's number."

"Do you have a pen?" he asked.

I peeked around the corner to the living room and grabbed a pen and paper from beside the phone cradle. I nodded, then realizing he couldn't see it, answered, "Yeah, I've got one."

He rattled off the number to me, then asked, "Where are Lucy and Max? You should all stick together."

"They're here," I answered, then after a moment of hesitation added, "Chase is here too."

There was silence on the other end of the line.

"Jason?" I questioned.

"Yes," he mumbled. "Yes I'm still here. It's good that he is there. You must stay together in your home. Don't go anywhere. Call Abel and I will be there as soon as possible."

I scrunched my nose in agitation. Like I couldn't have figured that all out on my own.

"Xoe?" Jason inquired.

"Yeah?"

"I love you."

My heart sped even faster, if that was possible. He'd never told me he loved me before. I had to clear my throat before I spoke. "I, um, I love you too."

"I will see you soon," he said. Then the line went dead.

I slumped back against the countertop, feeling like I had just run a marathon. Max was staring at me. "What?" I snapped.

He shook his head in exasperation. "Are you going to call Abel or what?"

I gave Max my best withering glare, though the tears probably lessened the effect. Boys can be so insensitive. I looked down at the forgotten paper in my hand. I glared back up at Max and dialed the numbers. A machine picked up after the first ring. A cultured woman's voice flowed out of the receiver, "Please leave your name, number, and a brief message." That was it, no explanation of whose machine I had reached. I just had to trust that I had the right number.

"Um, this is Xoe Meyers," I mumbled into the machine. "I'm trying to get a hold of Abel. I don't know if my dad already called, but we're having some trouble here in Shelby, the type of trouble that I think you are technically supposed to help us with." I gave the machine Max's cell phone number and hung up.

I let out a loud sigh to steady myself, then looked back to Max. "What are we going to do about Allison's parents? We're not supposed to get the police involved in this sort of stuff."

Max shrugged. "Maybe getting the cops involved wouldn't be such a bad thing. They might be able to help."

I shook my head; it *would* be much simpler if we could leave it to the cops, but we couldn't. It was supernatural commandment number one to keep humans uninvolved. Plus, if the cops were brought in we wouldn't get the coalition's help, and werewolves had a much better chance of finding Allison and Lela alive.

"We can't," I answered simply, too tired to explain my whole thought process.

Max cringed at my answer. "Well then what are we going to tell her parents?"

I pinched the bridge of my nose in frustration. "If we tell them anything, and we . . . " I choked on my words, emotion bubbling up anew, "and we can't find her," I managed to whisper, "then the cops will be knocking at our door."

Max looked up from where he had been gazing at the floor. "We can't tell her parents anything," he declared. "If they call the cops, then it's just humans calling human cops, and I still think it can't hurt to have them involved."

After a moment of silence I nodded. "You're right. Screw the rules. The coalition should have been up here trying to find the abductors as soon as that witch went missing in Bear Creek."

That elicited a small smile from Max. He gave me a light punch on the shoulder. "Now that's the Xoe we know and love."

I smiled back at Max. I left the phone on the counter and went through the dining room to bypass the living room on my way to the guest bathroom. Once inside, I did a quick mirror check to dry any leftover tears, then I went back to the living room.

127

My mom was leaning forward from her perch on the loveseat, grilling Chase about Greece of all things. Maybe I was right about where his accent was from. Max had resumed his seat next to Chase. I cleared my throat as I approached the seating area, drawing everyone's attention to me.

I met Chase's dark gray eyes. "Hey Chase," I began, "you think I could recruit you to help me wrap some Christmas presents? I don't want anyone to see what they got."

Chase nodded and smiled pleasantly at my mom before standing. I picked up some wrapping supplies from where my mom had put them near the tree. With the wrapping supplies under my arm, I headed upstairs with Chase following shortly behind, leaving Max and Lucy to fend off my mom.

As soon as we were shut inside my room, I spun on Chase. "Call my dad. Allison's missing. We can't just keep waiting around."

His eyes widened in surprise, but he pulled his cell phone out of his pocket and punched the buttons that would connect him to my dad. Chase's forehead scrunched in concern as my dad answered. "Their human friend is missing," Chase began without even a hello. He met my eyes. "I don't think your daughter will be content with sitting around and doing nothing for much longer."

I turned and looked out my large window while Chase listened to my dad. It took me a moment to realize that it was snowing outside. I huddled in my red sweater, even though it wasn't cold in my room. Chase clicked the phone shut and I turned my attention back to him.

"You're dad followed the woman from the coffee shop, but she just went to a bar afterwards. He saw another man watching her that he thinks isn't human, but the man simply followed her to the bar and is now waiting across the street. You're dad thinks they're being careful since we got away. They know we're on to them."

I scrunched my eyebrows together in concerned confusion. "Is this good or bad?"

Chase grimaced. "It could be good in the sense that they're possibly scared, which means that they are perhaps not as powerful as we think. But it's bad in the sense that their fear of exposure might cause them to rush. If Allison and Lela are alive, they may not be for much longer."

I dropped down onto my bed, feeling dizzy. This could not be happening, not again. When Lucy had been taken by Dan, I felt like the world was going to end, but at least then we had hope. We had Lela to lead us right to Lucy. We knew the bad guy we were dealing with.

"We have to go," I said numbly.

Chase shook his head. "We can't. We have no idea where they are."

"We have to get the woman," I countered. "She's our only lead."

"Kidnap the kidnapper?" Chase asked skeptically.

I glared at him. "You got a better idea?"

He shook his head. "We're not going to get by your dad. We'll have to convince him to help."

I smiled. "If I go after the woman, he won't really have a choice."

Chase stood and offered me a hand up from the bed. I took it gratefully, not caring if he knew how badly my knees were shaking. We were going into the den of the lion after all.

Here's hoping we didn't get bit.

Chapter Eleven

I left my room and crept as silently as I could down the stairs. My mom was still in the living room talking to Lucy and Max, so all of us just sneaking out wasn't an option. It was almost nine, so I knew my mom wouldn't allow us to go out that late. My only option was to have Max, and Chase "go home," then Lucy and I could sneak out. I'd have Lucy pretend to go home too, but it made more sense to have my mom think she was spending the night at our house, then if Lucy's parents called, we'd have a cover.

"You wanna stay the night Lucy?" I asked as I entered the room. Chase came into the room right behind me. I hadn't even realized that he'd been standing behind me on the stairs.

A look of confusion crossed Lucy's face, then she caught on. "Sure Xoe." She turned to my mom. "If that's okay with you."

"Of course!" My mom beamed. "You're always welcome. You know you don't have to ask."

Lucy smiled a little sickly. "I'll call my mom."

Chase brushed past me to face my mom. "Max and I better get going," he began. "Thanks for the cookies."

My mom turned her beaming smile towards Chase. She seemed to have settled back into her comfort zone, pretending we were all just a bunch of normal humans. Chase went for the door, then waited while Max said bye to my mom before heading out. My mom rejected our offers to help her clean up, so Lucy and I went up to my room.

"What's going on?" Lucy asked as soon as I shut my door.

"My dad followed the woman from the coffee shop to a bar. We're going to confront her, and quite possibly kidnap her."

Lucy's jaw dropped. "*What?*"

"Chase thinks that we might have spooked the abductors into acting. Whatever they're planning to do with Allison and Lela, they're probably going to rush into it now."

"So they do have Allison then?"

I nodded somberly. "I think so."

"But she's human," Lucy argued.

"I know," I replied. "I don't know why they took her too. Maybe she just got in the way."

"So we're sneaking out?"

I nodded. "As soon as my mom goes to sleep."

We went through the motions of getting ready for bed. I let Lucy borrow some pajamas, and by the time my mom peeked her head in to say goodnight, we were all tucked in and ready to "sleep".

We waited another twenty minutes to ensure that my mom was in bed, then, leaving the light off, got up and quietly changed back into our clothes. I pulled my slouchy boots back on, then added an insulated, waterproof black jacket to protect me from the cold. I tossed Lucy another winter coat and we were ready to go. Now for the tricky part.

Max and Jason usually just hopped out my second story window to sneak out of my room, but Lucy and I hadn't quite mastered that trick, despite the fact that we were supposed to be physically capable.

I peeked out my bedroom door to make sure we were all clear, then quickly pulled my head back in and shut the door as silently as possible. I turned to Lucy and whispered almost noiselessly, knowing she'd be able to hear, "She's still awake. Her door is open and her light is on."

Lucy grimaced. "What do we do?" she whispered back louder than I had. My hearing was good, but it was nowhere near werewolf hearing. They had me beat in the smell department too.

I glanced at my window and raised my eyebrows in question.

"No way," Lucy mouthed.

I looked at the window again, pursed my lips and nodded. We were going to do it. Ignoring Lucy's protests, I put some pillows under my comforter in case my mom glanced in my room, and slowly slid open my window.

Lucy came to stand beside me, sliding on the red winter coat I had given her. "No way, Xoe. We can't make it."

I ignored her and slid my feet out of the window, and braced myself to sit on the sill. I glanced back at Lucy's expression and held up my crossed fingers for her to see. I took a deep breath and pushed off against the side of the house. I was airborne for a brief freezing moment, then my feet hit the ground. My momentum sent me tumbling a few feet through the fresh snow to land on my side in a heap. I took a moment to survey how my body felt, and a smile crossed my face as I realized I was unharmed.

I stood and brushed the snow off my jeans, then turned to look up at my window. Lucy was still fully inside, a look of shock on her face. I did a little 'ta-dah' gesture, pointed at Lucy, then pointed at the ground beside me.

She shook her head and stepped back from the window. She raised her hands in a pushing 'no thanks' gesture. There was no way I had jumped out that window for nothing. I stomped my foot in frustration, and once again pointed at Lucy, then at the ground beside me.

After several more minutes of silent arguing, Lucy finally eased her feet out the window and sat on the sill like I had. She reached behind her to slide the window closed as much as she could while still leaving room for her butt on the sill.

Finally, she closed her eyes and I watched her face, knowing she was counting to three. Then she threw herself away from the house. She dropped straight down with her long hair flowing above her head, and landed lightly on her feet, dipping into a crouch to lessen the impact on her legs. I swore out loud, that was *so* not fair.

I pouted while I waited for Lucy to come stand beside me, then we started towards the road where we would meet Max and Chase. My mind raced with what we were about to do. I wished Jason was with us despite myself.

Chase's old, beat-up truck was already waiting for us by the time we reached the road. I opened the passenger door to a blast of heated air, then waited for Lucy to climb in ahead of me. She chose to sit in the middle of the front seat again, rather than in the back jump-seat with Max.

We were all silent as Chase put the truck in drive and headed towards town. I fidgeted around anxiously until I couldn't keep my mouth shut any longer.

"Okay," I began. "So here's what I'm thinking. I go in and talk to the redhead, and let her lure me wherever. You guys stay out of sight, then follow us."

"So you'd be like . . . bait?" Lucy squeaked.

"No," Max interjected. "I'll do it."

I turned around so I could meet his scared eyes. "Why should you do it? I'm your pack leader after all. I'm supposed to protect you."

Max sighed. "You're only our pack leader in name Xoe. We don't actually expect you to protect us. Plus, they've only taken witches, werewolves, and merpeople. They may not even want you."

"He's right," Chase added. "The plan has a better chance of working if Max goes in."

Pouting, I hunched down in my seat and glared out the front window as we exited onto the highway. Lucy cleared her throat and I turned to regard her.

"Aren't we forgetting something?" Lucy asked rhetorically.

I cocked my head in confusion at the same time Max asked, "What?"

"That woman is in a bar," she reminded us. "None of us can get into a bar."

"I can," Chase countered.

I turned to him in confusion. "How old are you anyways?"

"Twenty-two," he answered simply.

Lucy cleared her throat again. "That still brings us back to the problem of having a demon go in."

"I can get into a stupid bar," Max mumbled petulantly.

I turned back to Max. "You willing to try?"

He met my eyes, showing me the raw fear shining through. "Yes," he agreed.

Chase shook his head in disbelief. "Okay," he conceded. "We'll try."

The rest of the drive was a short one. We didn't know which bar the redhead was at, so we'd park in the same lot as before, and look for my dad.

The bar traffic was in full swing, so we had to search for a while before we found a spot. Chase backed into the spot, for a quick get-away I assumed, and shut off the engine. I opened the door and hopped out just before the cold air really hit me. Sporadic snowflakes had begun to fall once again, and I wished I was back in my house, having cookies and coffee with my mom.

I snuggled the zipper on my winter coat all the way up to my throat and waited for Lucy to get out behind me. Chase and Max came around the truck to fetch us.

"We stick together," Chase ordered. "It may take us a little longer to find Alexondre, but we can't risk another one of us being taken."

I shrugged. "Why don't you just *sense* him?"

Chase grimaced. "He can block me."

A faint wash of hope ran through me, tainted by my current, more pressing fears. "So I could in theory block him?"

Shrugging, Chase answered, "In theory maybe, but it takes a very powerful demon to be able to do so. I've only heard of pureblood demons having the ability."

"Can't we just call him?" Max interrupted, impatient to get the show on the road. "It's freezing out here."

I answered before Chase could. "He's not going to tell us where he is. He didn't want us to come."

Max nodded and we all began to walk towards the sidewalk. Without discussion, we strolled up the street towards Blue Moon, trying to act casual and inconspicuous. The streets were full of bar-goers and a few lingering coffee shop patrons with laptops or books in hand. People who would normally seem innocuous to me, all suddenly had hidden agendas of nefarious deeds. Was that woman in the black velvet coat looking at me funny? I stepped a little closer to Lucy, wanting to feel the comfort of being in a group.

We were only a block away from the coffee shop when Chase took a sudden right, and gestured for us all to cluster into an alcove that housed an ATM. We all smushed in and looked at him curiously. He gestured with a nod down the street we had just turned onto.

I peeked around the corner and saw my dad, leaning against a wall a few buildings down. As I watched, he pulled a cell phone out of his black linen trench coat and dialed a number. A second later, Chase's phone began to ring.

Chase cringed and reached into his pants pocket, then held the cell phone out to me. I flipped it open and held it to my ear. "I told you to stay home Alexondra," my dad's voice lectured.

I shut the phone and handed it back to Chase. He looked at me wide-eyed as I flipped my hood up over my head and left the alcove, marching straight for my dad. He pretended not to notice me as I walked down the street to meet him.

I stopped and leaned against the wall a few feet away from him. "Max is going in," I whispered. If there were any werewolves around, they'd probably hear me, but it was the best I could do.

My dad nodded; the barest inclination of his head. "You are staying out here with me," he whispered.

It was my turn to nod. I looked back towards the alcove to see Max emerging. Good, they were putting the plan into action. I casually tugged my hood down my forehead a little further, trying to mask my blonde hair in case one of the abductors recognized me.

There wasn't anyone checking IDs at the door, and Max strode right in. I waited, expecting Max to be thrown out any minute, but nothing happened. Another five minutes went by. Still nothing.

I glanced around to see if anyone else was watching the bar and caught site of Chase as he crossed the street. He had produced a black winter cap from somewhere, and pulled it down a little further over his ears as he sat down on a park bench and started pretending to text on his phone. Or who knew? Maybe he was texting.

I got my answer when my dad's phone buzzed from somewhere within his trench coat. He pulled out the phone and quickly read the message. He began to walk towards me as he shoved the phone back in his pocket. I ignored him until he placed a hand on my shoulder to turn me to walk with him.

"What's going on?" I whispered.

My dad pushed me forward to quicken our pace. "Max and the woman are behind the bar."

"Already?" I whispered harshly.

"He must have followed her straight out there as soon as he entered," my dad explained. "It was a trap."

I glanced to the park bench where Chase was sitting, but he had already disappeared. Standing in his place was the crew-cut man that had followed us before. He watched my dad and me as we crossed the street. Crap.

I stopped suddenly on the median to tie my shoe and my dad came to a skidding halt. I looked up and met his eyes that so eerily matched mine. "He's one of them, the one standing by the bench."

My dad glanced at the man, then pulled me to my feet to stroll a little more slowly the rest of the way across the road. We made our way to a little alley that ran alongside the bar. I glanced back in search of crew-cut man. He was walking right towards us. Double-crap.

My dad shoved me into the alleyway ahead of him, then stayed where he was standing. I looked at him, confused.

"Go," he ordered. "Find Chase." Then he turned to meet crew-cut man head on.

I went. I could only hope that crew-cut man wouldn't try anything too drastic in public.

I ran full out down the alleyway until I reached the back parking lot of the bar. I felt a prickling at the back of my neck. I whipped around and looked back down the alleyway. My dad was nowhere to be seen. I turned back around and was shocked to find dark brown eyes, just inches from my face.

I froze, heart thundering a million miles a minute. Then I realized that it was Nick standing in front of me. "You scared me!" I exclaimed.

He just stood there as a slow smile crept across his face.

Only then did it dawn on me that we hadn't told Nick where we were going. I started to back up, but for every step I took back, he took one forward. "You're one of them," I accused.

His smile grew as he continued to walk forward.

I turned to run, and caught a glimpse of someone large behind me. Then there was only darkness.

Chapter Twelve

I could hear an engine humming, trying to lull me back to sleep, but there was a dull ache in my head that told me I needed to wake up. I opened my eyes, but couldn't lift my head off the floor. I groggily looked around at my metal surroundings and realized I was in the back of a van. Wait, what was I doing in the back of a van?

Suddenly Nick's face was once again in front of mine and it all came flooding back to me. The traitor! I tried to speak, but it felt like my mouth was full of cotton.

Nick's face disappeared. A moment later I heard him speak. "She's coming to."

A woman's voice responded, "What the hell is she? Her metabolism has eaten up enough tranqs to down three werewolves."

Tranquilizers? This was bad, very bad. I began to struggle, but my limbs felt like they were made of rubber, and there was some type of restraint holding my hands behind my back. I managed to swing my leg enough to kick someone, then there were hands holding down my legs. I took a breath to try and scream, then there was a small zing of pain in my arm. My vision began to go dark. I blinked against it; I had to stay awake. Then I was out.

When I next awoke, I was in some sort of cell. The ground beneath me was cold, damp stone. I forced my eyes open only to find someone crouching over me. I swung my leg up as best I could in an attempt to kick whoever it was. My knee made contact, instead of my foot like I had intended, and the person fell away with a yelp.

"What gives?" a female voice demanded.

"Allison?" I questioned.

"Duh," came a sarcastic reply. "Don't try to kick me this time."

She crouched back over me and put her hands under my arms to lift me into a seated position. She leaned me against the stone wall, then sat down in front of me. I felt a wash of heat and glanced to see a small propane heater in the corner of the room, near the door, which I couldn't really think of as a door. It was made of shiny, new steel bars. There was some sort of lighting in the outer room, but the only extra lighting in the cell was the glow of the space heater.

I turned my gaze back to Allison, who was dressed in a dirty, long sleeve tee that had once been a pale blue, and torn jeans that had soaked up blood from some sort of wound or cut on her leg. It pained me somehow to see Allison this way; she always put so much effort into her clothing.

I looked at her bloody leg again. "What happened?"

Allison grimaced. "I just woke up with it. Some kind of puncture wound, but not too deep."

I forced my eyes up to focus in on her grime-smeared face to ask another question. "Where are we?"

"We don't know. We just woke up here."

I was about to ask who "we" was, but then I saw Lela. She was huddled in the far corner with her arms wrapped around her knees. Her head was hanging forward, causing her long dark hair to fall around her like a cape.

"Lela?" I questioned.

"Hi Xoe," Lela whispered back, clearly freaked out.

I looked back to Allison. "What did they do to her?" I whispered, even though I knew Lela would hear.

Allison shook her head. "She's claustrophobic. We think we're underground."

Come to think of it, there did seem to be a slight lack of air. Not enough to harm us, but still uncomfortable. There was a familiar sensation prickling at the back of my mind. The air felt heavy, like something was pressing down on me. Then it hit me where I had felt that feeling before. Lucy's grandma's funeral.

"We're in the cemetery . . . under the cemetery."

Allison's honey brown eyes widened. "We're where?"

I licked my lips nervously. "I um . . . I think we're in a crypt."

"Great, just great," another voice said sarcastically.

Wait, I knew that voice. "Brian?" I questioned.

Brian crawled into my line of vision and sat in front of me. His gray hoodie was torn and his hair was mussed into a frizzy pouf, but other than that, he looked unharmed. "So we're in a crypt huh?"

I cringed at his tone, then nodded in affirmation. "What are you doing here?" I asked.

Brian shrugged, an unpleasant, sour look on his face. "First I ran into you on the street, then, as soon as you walked away, some guy pulled me into an alley. The next thing I knew, I was waking up . . . in a crypt."

Lela let out a small whimper. My limbs tingled as feeling returned to them. Unfortunately the feeling was returning to my head as well. I reached back and felt the tender lump that had erupted on my scalp.

Allison and Brian were both staring at me.

"Have either of you seen anyone since you woke up?" I asked.

Allison was first to answer. "Yeah, Nick. The little worm told us if we used any magic, they'd know. Apparently nobody bothered to tell him that I'm human, so he just assumed otherwise." She scowled at the room in general and then added, "They don't know what you are either Xoe."

"You'd think he would have just asked, back when we trusted him."

Allison nodded. "Yeah, not the sharpest tool in the shed that one."

"He did ask," Lela interrupted from her corner. "I told him it was your choice if and when you wanted to tell him."

I flashed back on Lela's googly-eyed look for Nick. That she had kept my secret despite her feelings for him pushed Lela that last inch into my friend category. If we got out of this, I knew I could trust her.

I gave Lela a smile she didn't see, then turned back to Allison. "I understand them not knowing my smell, but wouldn't they know that you smell human?" I asked.

"Witches smell like humans, unless they've been doing a lot of magic." Lela interjected softly.

Brian was absorbing our conversation with a look of confused wonder on his face. I spared him an apologetic smile, then turned to regard Lela again. "Did you recognize what any of them smelled like?" I asked.

"Nick is definitely a wolf," Lela said sadly. "The other one I caught a whiff of had a smell I knew. Kind of like the smell right before it rains mixed with blood."

"Like ozone maybe?" I asked. "That's what Max said one of them smelled like."

Lela gave a slight nod of her head in answer. "Dan smelled the same way when after he summoned demons. He said it was from the magic."

"Great, just great," I replied. "So do we have any idea what they're planning on doing with us?"

"Kill us, probably," Lela mumbled.

Brian put his head in his hands, but didn't say anything.

I wanted to argue, but Lela was right. All but one of the other abductees were yet to be found, and the one that was found was dead.

Allison glanced at the door, then back to me. "Can't you blow it up or something?"

I raised my hand to pinch the bridge of my nose. I was getting a killer headache. "I don't know how," I groaned. "I've only blown up appliances, so I think it just has something to do with the electricity."

"What about the space heater?" Lela asked, a little bit of the strength back in her voice.

I looked at the heater again. It wasn't electric, but it was flammable. "You might just have something there."

I stumbled to my feet and Allison stood to aide me. "How did you get over the tranquilizers so fast? It took over an hour for Lela to be able to move at all. I was on the ground for another two after that. Brian finally just started moving before they threw you in here."

"Who threw me in?" I asked.

Allison shrugged. "Some big guy," she answered. "I'd never seen him before."

Brian lifted his head out of his hands and looked at me standing awkwardly near the door. "What are you going to do?"

I shook my head and glanced at the heater again. "I don't know. Can one of you help me move the space heater by the bars?"

Allison left me leaning against the wall as she went to move the heater. It was a lot heavier than it looked, so she had to slowly drag it across the floor rather than lifting it. It made a horrible scraping sound its entire journey to the door.

At the noise, a tall man with icy blue eyes and hair so blonde it was almost white came around the corner into view through the barred door. He was also the largest man I had ever seen. When he spoke, his voice was a deep bass rumble. "What was that noise?" he asked with what sounded like a German accent.

"What noise?" I asked back.

"That scraping."

"Oh," I began, trying to think of an excuse. "We, um . . . we wanted to move the heater. We figured if we moved it in front of the door, less heat would escape. Where's my dad?"

It took him a moment to adjust to my train of conversation. He was big, and none too bright.

Before he could answer, I asked, "What about the rest of my friends?"

"There are only you four," he responded. He turned to walk away.

"Hold on," I urged. "Why are we here?"

He stopped mid-motion and faced me again. "I'm not supposed to tell you."

"What happened to my leg?" Allison quickly added.

The big man had the grace to look embarrassed. "I dropped you. There was a sharp piece of glass on the ground."

Lela began to weep softly.

The big man pointed at her. "What's wrong with that one?"

I couldn't think of a reason not to tell him, and I wanted to keep him talking, so I answered honestly. "She's claustrophobic."

"Claude!" someone shouted from the outer room.

Claude winced, gave me a surprisingly sympathetic look, and walked away.

Back to the space heater idea. I motioned for Allison and Brian to stand back with Lela, then stumbled to sit several feet in front of the space heater. I stared into the glowing red panel, trying to grasp at my elusive powers, and felt . . . nothing.

I continued to stare, waiting for something to happen.

147

"What's wrong?" Allison whispered.

"I don't know," I answered. "I don't know how to do it."

"Don't you have to, you know, get angry?"

I shrugged. "I guess so, but I don't have much anger right now. I'm leaning more towards scared out of my wits."

"Think about something that makes you mad," Allison urged.

"I'm trying," I hissed.

"Try harder!" she shouted.

I whipped my head around to glare at her.

She put her hands up in surrender. "Sorry, just trying to make you mad."

I pouted, realizing that she almost had me when I ruined it.

"Xoe?" Brian questioned, letting his fear trickle into his voice. "What are you trying to do?"

"Nothing," I snapped without looking back at him.

"Can you believe Nick?" Allison interrupted. "He had us all fooled."

"Yeah, the weasel," I responded grumpily.

"He even gloated about it," she went on. "Said he couldn't believe how easily we let him in. That we were naïve and stupid to trust him like that."

I sighed loudly, depressed. "We were."

"So get mad about it," Allison urged.

"I can be mad about my own failure, but it's not something I'm going to lose my temper over."

"What are you trying to do?" Brian shouted.

I spun around to regard his scared, angry face. "Nothing!" I snapped again.

"Oh, and he said one more thing," Allison went on. "He told me that he could take you on with both hands tied behind his back."

"Stop it Allison!" Brian yelled. "What are you guys trying to do?"

"SHUT . . UP!" I shouted.

That was the spark I needed. I felt a thrill of electricity zing through my body, and suddenly the space heater exploded. It exploded . . . a little too much. A whoosh of roiling fire surrounded me, then in an instant was gone.

I waited for the pain to hit, and felt . . . nothing. I looked down at my hands, sure that I had to be burned, but they were their normal smooth whiteness.

"That hurt," Allison said from behind me.

Uh oh. I stood up, feeling numb, and rushed to the corner where my friends had taken shelter. I crouched in front of them to survey the damage.

"I'm so sorry!" I exclaimed when I saw them.

Allison's eyes were wide with shock. Allison held her hands up to her face, but didn't touch her skin. "Is it bad?"

"No, um, not too bad," I answered. "You just look kinda . . . pink"

"I feel like I'm sunburned," Brian added.

I heard shouting from the outer room. "Um guys," I prompted, "we gotta go."

Allison pushed against the wall to slowly get to her feet. I had to grab Lela's hand and pull her up to get her moving. "What do we do?" Lela shouted, only now snapping back to reality. The shouting was getting closer.

Thinking quickly, I answered, "We've got to make way for Allison or Brian to get away. They can tell the others where we are."

With that I turned and ran to the cell door. The heater hadn't actually done much damage, but it had broken the lock and latch, and one of the bottom hinges. The corner of the door scraped harshly against the stone floor as I pulled it open. The metal felt warm to the touch, but didn't burn, either because it had cooled, or because I was a demon. At the moment, I didn't really care.

I entered the larger stone room. It was almost as barren as our cell had been. A couch, mini-fridge, and another space heater were the only things in the empty space, plus another make-shift cell next to ours. Oh, and Claude. He had probably come to investigate the shouting and ended up too close to the blast. His large form was curled on the ground in agony, but it seemed like he'd live. I caught a single glimpse of his charred face, then extinguished my pang of guilt to turn my attention to the footsteps coming down a small stone staircase.

The first of our abductors to enter the room was Nick. I felt a smile spread across my face. We had to make our way out, and if I had to go through a person to do that, I was very glad that it was Nick.

He stood on the stairs, looking stunned to see all four of us out of our cell. He recovered quickly, and crouched into what looked like a professional fighting stance. I nervously tried to recall how I had blown up the space heater, but before I could do anything, Lela leapt on Nick with a shriek of anger. They tumbled sideways off the stairs to land in a writhing heap on the stone floor.

Lela ended up on top. I watched in terrified amusement as she cocked back one dainty fist, then started pummeling Nick in a blur of motion. Shakespeare was right; hell hath no fury like a woman scorned.

Deciding that Lela could handle Nick, I grabbed Allison and shoved her up the stairs ahead of me, then pulled Brian up behind me. We emerged into a small room that was thankfully above ground. There was no door, just a large frame leading out into the moonless night. We were close to freedom.

Just then, crew-cut man stepped into the doorway, blocking the entire opening with his broad shoulders. Lela came trotting up the stairs to stand slightly behind me.

"It's four to one," I said to the crew-cut man. "I suggest you move unless you want to end up like your friends."

"I don't think so," said a voice from behind the crew-cut man. The big man stepped through the doorway to reveal a tiny blonde woman. A tiny blonde woman with a gun.

She flipped her shoulder-length hair out of her face, then gestured with her gun that we should walk back down the stairs.

"That one stays up here," the big man said pointing to Allison.

The blonde woman gave him an angry glance, then gestured once again that we should go downstairs.

"They have Megan," he argued.

"You knew the risks when you took my money," blondie answered sharply.

"Kidnapping teenagers wasn't part of the deal. I'm going to get Megan back, then we're going to disappear.

"A trade?" the blondie asked without looking at him.

The man nodded and started to walk towards Allison.

"They'll never go for it," blondie taunted. "They won't trade just for one and let us keep the others."

"I have to try," the big man said angrily.

"Fine, try," she snapped. "But not yet. Take her somewhere, then go and offer them the trade in the morning. Just make sure they don't actually get her back until after tomorrow night. She turned back to Lela and me. "You two, back downstairs."

What else could we do? Lela might survive a couple gun shots, heck I might too. I didn't really want to find out, but apparently Lela did. She leapt at the woman, completely ignoring the gun pointed right at her chest. The woman froze too long and didn't get a chance to shoot. They both tumbled out the doorway.

Allison took the opportunity to slip the big man's grasp and run for the door as well. He turned to go after her and I leapt onto his back, trying to buy her a few minutes. He struggled to reach his meaty arms behind his back to grab me, then finally just slammed his back against the wall, crushing the air out of me. I slid off his back to land in a crouch, wincing at what was probably a broken rib.

As I tried to re-learn how to breathe, Brian came up behind the big man. He hefted a broken two-by-four he had found somewhere and swung it like a baseball bat to hit the man across the back of the head. The man barely flinched, then turned on Brian and swatted him as if he was an annoying insect. Brian went sailing right out the doorway. This guy was so obviously not human.

From my position on the ground, I lunged and grabbed the man's ankle. I was plenty mad now, and my powers came flowing easily through me. The smell of burning flesh crept up to my nostrils just as the man screamed and fell away from me. I lost my grip on his ankle as he tucked his feet beneath him to end up in a crouch.

Brian limped back into view. "Run!" I screamed.

I turned my attention back to crew-cut man. His eyes glazed with rage, he lunged for me again. I managed to evade his grip and made a dash for the door. I could see Lela and Allison running away in the distance, Brian leapt out the door to follow behind them. I couldn't blame them for leaving me. If at least one of us could get away, they could get help for whoever couldn't.

As the cool night air enveloped me, I began to think that maybe all four of us would get away. Then in my peripheral vision I saw the blonde woman, limping and with blood running down her face. With a truly terrifying grin, she lifted the rock that was in her hand.

For the second time that night, I was out like a light.

Chapter Thirteen

I stumbled into consciousness, fighting the familiar feeling of tranquilizers. I was in what seemed like a hotel room this time. I could feel the scratchy synthetic comforter under my hands. That was about all I had time to notice before the blonde woman's scraped and bruised face appeared above mine.

"I don't think so," she whispered. I felt another sting in my arm. The last thought I had before my eyelids fluttered shut was that I was going to die.

When I finally came to the next time, it was night again. Now if only I knew which night it was. My first thought was that I was absolutely freezing. I hung by my arms against what felt like a large tree. My winter coat was missing and the rough bark scraped against my back as I struggled to free myself. I looked down as best I could to see that my feet were about two feet from the ground.

The smell of smoke was thick in the air, scented with what smelled like cinnamon and anise. I crinkled my nose in distaste as the cloying scent stuck in my sinuses. I hate anise. As more of my conscious thought returned,

I began to survey my surroundings. A large cracked piece of stone was only a few feet away from where I hung. I had to swallow past a lump in my throat when I realized what it was . . . a gravestone.

Panicking, I began to struggle more against my restraints, which felt like they were made of metal. The graveyard was the last place I wanted to wake up. Well, the last place besides an actual grave. I mentally mapped out the Shelby graveyard, trying to place what area I was in. There were simply too many trees around though. The graveyard had trees, but they were spaced farther apart than the trees I was currently surrounded by.

I had to be somewhere in the woods. There were old abandoned houses in the woods; it would only make sense that those who lived there would have had a graveyard. A really old graveyard. This was very, very bad.

I worked against the bonds on my hands some more, but only succeeded in scraping and probably bloodying my wrists. My arms and shoulders ached from supporting the weight of my body. I took a deep breath to try and scream.

I found I could scream, but was cut off quickly as someone suddenly appeared out of the darkness in front of me. It was the psychotic, gun-toting blonde. So, I was officially in the last place I wanted to be, staring down at the last person I wanted to see. Heck, I'd even take Nick over her.

"Hello again," she said cheerfully.

I glared down at her, not saying anything. She had a black eye and deep scratches running down one side of her face.

"Don't wanna talk huh?" she asked. She smiled a truly wicked smile. "That's okay," she went on. "You don't have to talk. All we need is your blood."

My blood? Crap, crap, crap, crap, crap. I swung my foot out in an attempt to kick her in her smug little face, but she easily dodged to the side and out of reach. She laughed a horrible jingling little laugh that I would remember forever (however long forever might be) and walked away.

I didn't have to wait alone for long. Nick came swaggering into sight to stand several feet away from me. His air of superiority was slightly tainted by his battered face, courtesy of Lela. Unfortunately his werewolf blood had already healed the bruises to an ugly yellow.

"Afraid to get too close?" I mocked.

"Not afraid," he countered. "Just smart."

"That's debatable," I mumbled.

"What the hell are you anyway?" he asked. "I saw what you did to Claude and Michael."

Michael must have been crew-cut man's name. "I'll tell you what I am," I offered, "if you tell me what the heck you plan to do with me."

"We plan to slit your throat and steal your powers," he stated calmly.

His words hit me like a ton of bricks. I mean, I knew they were planning to kill me, but hearing it put so coldly put ice in my veins. "Did you steal the others' powers? The ones you abducted?" I asked weakly.

"Yep," he answered cheerfully. "I mean, I was already a werewolf, but Jaime promised to give me more powers if I helped her get hers. She promised me *your*

157

powers, and now that I've seen what you can do, I'm very glad that she did."

Okay, I thought, *keep him talking; buy more time.* "Jaime?" I asked. "Is that the blonde? How does she do it? Steal the powers I mean."

He traced the toe of his shoe in the dirt absentmindedly. "I dunno," he answered. "She lights the funny smelling fire and calls to . . . something. As far as I can tell, it's like a spirit or something. You'll see. It appears in the fire. Then she slits our captive's throat. That would be you," he pointed a despicable finger at me. "Then she puts your blood into a big bowl and pours it into the fire for the spirit thingy. As far as I can tell, the spirit takes the powers from the blood, and gives them to her or to whoever she tells it to."

I was getting dizzy. I had to swallow back the bile that was climbing up my throat to ask, "If all you need is blood, can't you just take it from a non-lethal place. You can have my powers," I pleaded. "I don't want them."

"Nope," he said with a smile. "The spirit says that the captive has to die before it can take their powers. It has to separate them from your soul. Now that's enough explanation. Tell me what you are."

"I'm something you really don't want to mess with," I threatened.

He laughed at that. "Sorry honey. Threats don't really work when you're tied to a tree."

I forced myself to smile back at him, but it was more just a baring of teeth. "Remember when we met?" I asked. "And I told you I'd kill you if you betrayed me?"

He nodded. "Yep. It makes this situation all the more gratifying."

Ignoring his lack of fear I went on. "Well," I began, "I may not be able to kill you myself, but you'll still end up just as dead."

"And how's that?" he asked, still smiling.

"Because of what I am," I answered. "I'm a demon, which in and of itself might not deter you, but demons run together, and you *so* don't want demons after you."

"Get out of town," he said jovially. "A demon? Yours' have to be like, the coolest powers ever."

"You are such an idiot," I mumbled, losing hope.

"We'll see about that," he remarked, then disappeared back into the darkness.

"We'll see about that," I mimicked to myself as he left. My wrists were throbbing from the restraints cutting into them. I had to get out of here. I closed my eyes and focused, trying to muster even a spark of fire to do . . . something. If I could blow up appliances, maybe I could melt the metal restraints. Or maybe set the tree branch I was hanging from on fire?

I tried to focus on how mad I should be at the whole situation, at Nick's casual talk about my death, but all I could feel was tired and scared.

I heard chanting behind me, from where I assumed the fire was. I was running out of time. What the heck kind of spirit steals powers only to give them back to a mortal anyhow? Was death what it wanted? That didn't really sound like a spirit. As far as I knew spirits didn't have, nor did they care about, that kind of power. No, this particular deal sounded more like a demon. Not all demons are good ya know.

There was a loud whoosh, and I shuddered with the sudden electric sensation. The demon was here.

159

"Where is it?" I heard Nick's voice ask.

"I don't know," Jaime answered sharply. "Just shut up."

The demon wasn't here? But I had felt it . . .

"Maybe it ran away scared," another voice chimed in.

A surge of hope washed through me when I realized that it was my dad's voice. The whoosh had come from him! I smiled deliriously and tried to struggle against my restraints again. Then the screaming started.

Jaime screamed first, followed shortly by Nick. I watched in awe as glowing shadows decorated the forest in front of me from the flames. The screaming didn't last long. A few moments later, my dad came walking around my tree to stand before me.

"Hello Alexondra!" he said cheerfully. He stood at ease with his hands in the pockets of his slacks, no sign of stress on his face for having just killed two people.

"Hi dad," I answered, then cringed when I realized that I had called him dad. I'd been doing it in my head so much lately that it just came out.

He pretended not to notice my slip up as he set about examining the tree I was hanging from. Apparently seeing no other way, he hoisted himself up into the tree by some of the lower branches. I waited anxiously as his feet disappeared into the foliage.

"You ready?" He asked.

"Just do it," I grumbled.

With a loud snap, the branch I was hanging from broke off and I fell to the ground in a heap. My dad thrust the branch off to the side as he let it drop so it wouldn't land on me.

I stayed on the ground where I had landed, not quite ready to move. My dad's feet landed right beside my head, then he was hoisting me up with his hands beneath my shoulders. Now that I was down, he took a closer look at my cuffs. "Wait here," He ordered, then disappeared around the tree.

I stumbled after him, feeling like I somehow needed to see the carnage, if only to assure myself that it was really over. I expected a rather grisly scene, but it wasn't all that bad. Was the fact that I could think of two charred corpses as 'not all that bad' a bad sign?

Don't answer that.

My dad kicked the smaller of the blackened corpses, making parts of it disintegrate into ash. He walked a few steps away from the corpse, apparently spotting what he was looking for, then came up with a purse in his hand. Jaime's purse. Luckily she hadn't been holding it when, well, you know.

He dug through it and came out with a set of keys. He tossed the purse into Jaime's fire as he walked back to me. He shuffled through the key ring and separated the handcuff key from the rest.

He stuck the key into my cuffs and they blissfully fell from my hands, one wrist, then the other.

"What took you so long?" I asked. "I thought you could *sense* me."

He furrowed he brow in annoyance. "I cannot *sense* you when you are underground or unconscious. Tonight was the first time you were awake long enough for me to get a mark on you."

I glanced down at Jaime's fire. "What happened to the other demon?"

My dad chuckled. "Turns out I know that particular demon. He has the ability to temporarily grant powers to people. It's a game that he plays."

"So what?" I asked. "He takes powers, gives them to people, then takes them back?"

My dad nodded.

"But why?" I asked.

My dad shrugged. "Why not? He thinks it's fun. Convince people to kill supernaturals. Once he's had his fun he kills the people he originally made the deal with."

My jaw dropped in stunned understanding. I had almost died because of a . . . joke? "You're kidding. It's all for nothing? That is just . . . sick."

He grinned like the proverbial crocodile. "Not all demons are good you know."

I shrugged of the thought that he had echoed my earlier thoughts exactly. He grabbed my left arm and draped it across his shoulder, and I let him, because my knees were going to give out any minute.

"You know, I still hate you," I said, needing to reassure myself of that fact.

"Yes Alexondra, I know," he answered, only the slightest mocking to his tone.

I looked down at Nick's corpse. "I told you so," I mumbled to it.

"What?" my dad asked.

"Nothing," I answered. "Will I be able to do that someday?" I asked, gesturing to the remains.

"Oh yes Alexondra. I have very high hopes for you," he answered.

Now *that* juicy little tidbit, was most definitely a bad thing. A very, very, *very* bad thing indeed.

Chapter Fourteen

I found out that my dad could take me with him when he teleported, though he scoffed at the word teleportation. He called it simply "traveling."

Whatever it was called, I was soon out of the forest. I assumed we would be going to my house, but in the blink of an eye, we were in the parking lot of Jason's apartment instead. My dad basically carried me up the stairs, though I pretended to walk as much as possible. Jason flung open his door before we could even knock.

He lifted my arm from my dad's shoulder and took me into a crushing hug. "I got here as soon as I could," he breathed into my hair. "I'm so sorry. I should have never left."

"No, you shouldn't have," I mumbled. I ignored the painful protest of my bruised ribs and let Jason continue crushing me.

I felt wetness against my cheek and realized he was crying. He drew me farther into his apartment, leaving the door open for my dad to come in. Jason sat me down on his generic apartment couch, then sat close beside me.

I looked questioningly at my dad as he hovered awkwardly above us. He nodded towards Jason. "He made me promise to bring you straight here."

I rolled my head to the side to look at Jason. "He would not let me come," he explained, sounding a bit petulant.

My dad sighed loudly. "I *also* told him that I can only carry one person when I travel, I needed to be able to carry Alexondra back."

"And I told him . . . " Jason began.

I cut him off with a hand in the air, but forgot what I was going to say when I got my first good look at my wrists. They had partially healed already, but were still a sickening greenish brown, with ugly scabs decorating where the cuffs had worn away my skin.

At that moment Chase, Lucy, Allison, Max, Lela, and even Brian came bursting into Jason's apartment. At my startled expression, Jason explained, "I called them when your dad left to get you."

Lucy and Allison were the first to crush me with their hugs. "You *stink*," Allison remarked as she slowly pulled away.

Her remark made me giggle. Then that giggle turned into full out, gut-churning laughter. My friends stared at me as if I had just recited the *Bhagavad-Gita*, and I laughed all the more. I was probably delirious with shock and exhaustion, and I didn't care in the least. We had once again come out of things alive.

My laughter ended just as abruptly as it started, as a truly horrifying thought dawned on me. "What did you guys tell my mom?"

No one answered me.

"Well?" I prompted.

"They *drugged* her," Brian answered.

My jaw dropped as I met Brian's serious brown eyes. I turned to Allison, seeing as she was the only other one who would meet my eyes. "You drugged my mom?" I asked skeptically.

Allison cringed. "Um, your dad did it."

I turned my attention to the demon in question. "Care to explain?"

"I didn't *drug* her," he responded, his voice betraying not the slightest drop of guilt. "I gave her something to make her sleep, and to make her memory a little . . . foggy."

"You drugged my mom!" I shouted.

My dad cocked his head and gave me a look that said I was being very silly. "What would you rather I had done?"

I was left once again with my mouth hanging open like an idiot. "I don't know, but you shouldn't have drugged her."

My dad just shrugged and began to casually explore Jason's apartment. I gave up on that particular argument and put my head in my hands. "What happened to the rest of our abductors?" I asked. I couldn't help flashing back to Claude's charred face. He'd seemed nice . . . for a kidnapper. The others could rot for all I cared.

"The red-haired woman will be dealt with," my dad answered. "The others have disappeared."

"Nick?" Lela asked sadly.

"Kindling," I answered.

She nodded and slumped down onto the couch next to me.

"Now, when you say she'll be 'dealt with,'" I began, turning my attention back to my dad, "what exactly does that mean?"

"Do you really care?" Chase asked before my dad could answer.

I regarded him with a scowl. "Yes, I care." Turning to my dad again I added, "Just don't kill her okay?"

My dad nodded sharply. "Okay."

Now that that was settled, on to the next emergency . . . I seriously stunk. "Can we go home now?" I whined. "I'm in dire need of a shower."

Jason took my arm to help me stand. I was still feeling shaky, so I let him. After days of blocking out how much I missed him, it felt good just to be near him again.

We silently left Jason's apartment, and I proceeded to wobble down the stairs to the parking lot. I managed to do it without much help from Jason thanks to my death-grip on the railing. The only other vehicle I recognized in the lot was Chase's, and I wondered how everyone had gotten to Jason's together.

In answer to my question, Lela stepped up beside me. "Mind if I ride with you and Jason?" She asked. "The ride over in that excuse for a truck was none too comfortable."

"Sure," I mumbled as I shuffled over to the passenger's side of Jason's car. Jason unlocked his car while the rest of my friends piled into Chase's truck. My dad came to stand beside me, preventing me from escaping to the safety of the car.

"You need to let me teach you Alexondra," he stated simply. Jason and Lela had already gotten inside the car, so I had no one to turn to for an interruption.

I glared up into my dad's expressionless face. I realized his nose was slightly sharper than mine, not as similar as the rest of our faces, and I took a brief moment to revel in that fact. "You could try actually asking me," I said finally. "And it's Xoe."

I expected him to roll his eyes at me, but he met my gaze seriously. "Please let me teach you . . . Xoe."

I closed my eyes and breathed in the crisp night air. This would be the final step to letting him into my life. "Fine," I mumbled.

He smiled, and it was genuine. "I will see you soon then."

I opened the car door, then turned to stop him before he disappeared. "Hey," I began, "I have a question."

He raised an eyebrow at me in response.

"When they kidnapped me, they gave me a bunch of tranquilizers," I explained, "but I got over them really quickly, faster than Lela did."

My dad chuckled to himself before answering. "You have enough oomph to create fire; a fast metabolism is part of the package."

I couldn't help my smile at the term "oomph." I liked it a lot better than "demon power." "Oomph huh?" I asked. "I guess I can deal with a little oomph," I conceded.

I slipped into the car just as my dad disappeared in a cloud of smoke. He apparently didn't care if anyone saw him. If only we all could be so secure.

Chapter Fifteen

When we got back to my house, Chase's truck was already parked out front. I wanted nothing more than to be alone with Jason, but my friends had been worried about me, and I could stand to spend a few minutes to reassure them that everything was really okay.

Jason, Lela, and I went into the house to find Max, Lucy, and Chase waiting in the living room. I went to stand near the couch with Jason following me like a shadow. No one said anything.

I stood awkwardly for a moment more. I was *way* too tired for this. "I'm, um, gonna go shower," I announced, pointing one finger half-heartedly towards the stairs. I hustled out of the living room and up the stairs, Jason never more than two steps behind me the entire way.

Once we were alone in my room, I fell into Jason's arms. I hadn't even checked to see if my mom was awake. I still had no idea what I was going to say to her. 'Sorry, but dad had to drug you.' I somehow didn't think that would go over too well. Maybe I'd be able to convince her that she'd hit her head, and was now suffering from a minor case of harmless amnesia.

Jason sat down on the bed, and I curled awkwardly into his lap. My legs were a little too long for it, but at the moment I needed to be as close to him as I could. His dark brown sweater was slightly scratchy and I found myself briefly wondering why scratchy sweaters even existed. Who buys scratchy sweaters when there are soft ones out there? Jason apparently. Okay, I was obviously still a bit delirious. What had I come upstairs for again?

As if reading my mind, Jason asked softly, "Are you going to shower?"

"Oh, um, yeah," I mumbled in reply.

When I didn't move, he lifted me easily so he could stand, then set me gently back on the bed. He leaned down by my head and kissed the side of my forehead. "I will get Lucy to help you," he whispered.

"No," I mumbled, "get Allison." Lucy would fuss over me nervously. Allison would take things in stride, and wouldn't make me feel pathetic about needing help to be bathed. I wanted to do it myself, but now that I was safe, my body simply wouldn't move anymore.

Jason left while I was still sorting through my muddled thoughts, and before I knew it, Allison was doing her best to make me stand up so she could help me into the bathroom. I didn't really help much. In fact, I think I might have blacked out a little, because the next thing I knew, I was slumping down into a nice, hot bath. Ah, heaven.

Allison sat on the closed toilet. I was glad to have her there. It would really suck to have survived all of the danger, only to pass out and drown in the tub.

Allison leaned her head in her hands tiredly. She was dressed in a pale pink cardigan and faded jeans that made her look delicate and out of place next to my dark purple décor. "I shouldn't have left you Xoe," she said, tears choking her voice. "I'm so sorry."

I sunk a little deeper into the hot water. Allison had rolled up a towel for me to lean my head against and I got it wet with my movement. Not caring, I sunk down until the water was at my chin. "I told you to leave Al," I mumbled.

"But it was so we could get help," she argued. "By the time we got back to the crypt, you were gone. We left you all alone and it didn't help at all."

"You did the right thing," I breathed tiredly. "Just let it go."

Allison nodded to herself, then changed the subject. "Jason didn't get back to Shelby until just after Lela, Brian, and I escaped. He went crazy when he found out you'd been taken. It took Max, Chase, and your dad to hold him down and keep him from running off on his own to look for you."

When I didn't answer, she continued to fill me in. "And that was after it apparently took Max, Lucy, and your dad to get Chase to the truck after they lost you at the coffee shop."

At that I raised a questioning eyebrow, but kept my eyes closed. "You know he's not going anywhere, now that the danger's over I mean."

"Who?" I asked, not able to follow her train of thought.

"Chase," she answered. "He views your dad as family. Now he's got this weird protective thing with you."

"Surely you jest," I mumbled, and smiled to myself. Yeah, I was definitely delirious.

Allison took me seriously. "I just had to spend an entire 24 hours with him and your dad when we were looking for you. Trust me when I say that neither of them is going anywhere."

I opened my eyes a crack to regard her. Come to think of it, she did look more than a little tired. "You guys haven't slept?" I asked.

"Of course not!" she squeaked, looking offended.

Okay, I hadn't realized I was making everyone wait when they hadn't slept at all the previous night. "Towel please," I asked.

I was feeling a little better, and managed to stand on my own while Allison held a towel open for me. I swaddled myself in its wonderful fluffy softness and stepped onto my purple rug, not caring that I was still dripping water from my legs. Allison pushed the little switch to drain my bathtub, then followed me into my bedroom. I sat on my bed while she pawed through my drawers. She threw me my dark green sweats and a long-sleeved black *Bauhaus* tee.

As soon as I was dressed, Allison helped me out of my room and back downstairs. We entered the living room to find Lucy, Lela, and Max all passed out. Lela and Lucy had taken the couches, so Max had simply taken a throw pillow and passed out on the floor. A wonderful smell was wafting out of the kitchen.

Allison walked over to lie on the floor by Max as I made my way to the kitchen. I found Jason and Chase leaning against the kitchen counter, each sipping on a mug of coffee. Seeing me, Jason went into the dining room and came back with a chair for me. I slumped into it gratefully then extended my hands for the mug of coffee Chase had poured for me.

"We threw in a couple of frozen pizzas," Jason informed me, "though I guess we're the only three eating now."

I nodded. "Is my mom still asleep?" I asked without looking up from my mug.

"Yes," Chase answered. "She should be out until morning."

I grimaced, still not liking the idea of my mom being drugged, though I had to admit, it was rather convenient.

When the pizzas were done, the three of us sat in the dining room and ate in silence. As soon as we finished, Chase stood. "I can take Max home if you want," he offered.

I nodded, still not saying anything. I watched as Jason went to wake the wolf in question, but he was out cold, so Jason simply lifted him and carried him outside.

Chase looked down at me once we were alone. "I guess, to sound horribly cliché, this is goodbye."

I thought of what Allison had said about him, and I thought about the fact that Chase didn't have a family. "Me and my mom always make a big dinner on Christmas eve. It's one of the few days out of the year that we actually cook. You should come."

Jason came back into the room before Chase could answer, so Chase simply smiled, then turned and walked out of the dining room. As soon as the door was shut, Jason sat down beside me again. "You invited him to Christmas Eve dinner?" he asked.

I crossed my arms and lowered my head to the table. "We needed another demon to round out the group," I mumbled.

"Am I supposed to know what that means?" Jason asked with a hint of laughter in his voice.

I shook my head, keeping my face buried in my arms and laughed despite my exhaustion. "It means it's bedtime," I answered.

A moment later, Jason hoisted me up in his arms and proceeded to carry me upstairs. I left Lucy, Allison, and Lela where they were. If they got cold, Lucy and Allison knew where the spare blankets were. Jason carried me into my room and placed me on bed.

I waited while he shut my bedroom door, then I felt him snuggle up beside me. We had a brief struggle of trying to put the comforter over us without actually getting off the bed. Then we settled in for me to sleep.

Ah, heaven.

Chapter Sixteen

I woke up at 6:00am; uncharacteristically early for me, especially given how exhausted I had been. I looked groggily around my room for Jason, only to realize that he wasn't there. I slipped out of bed and padded barefoot into my bathroom. There was an unpleasant looking ring around my tub from my bath the night before. I grabbed the foaming bathroom cleaner that I kept under my pedestal sink on the floor and gave the bathtub a good spray down and left it at that.

I gathered my hair into a ponytail, washed my face and brushed my teeth, then went in search of my mom. I found her milling around in her room, looking dazed and disoriented. She didn't even notice me watching her from the doorway.

"Just wake up?" I asked her.

She practically jumped out of her skin at my voice. She whipped around and saw that it was only me, and put her hand to her heart in relief. "You scared me to death honey," she breathed, then scrunched up her face in confusion.

"Are you feeling . . . okay?" I asked hesitantly.

She nodded and slumped down to sit on her bed. "It's the weirdest thing," she explained. "I can't remember yesterday at all, or the night before really. The last thing I remember was having cookies and cinnamon rolls with you and your friends."

Thanks a lot dad. "Um, did you hit your head or something?" I asked.

She cocked her head while she tried to come up with an answer. "I don't remember hitting it, but then again, if that's what made me lose my memory, I probably wouldn't remember it. I *do* have a killer headache."

"Do you want to go to the hospital?" I asked, keeping my fingers crossed that the answer would be no. There was no telling what they might find.

She shook her head, then answered, "I think I'm okay. I mean, besides the headache, my head isn't actually sore anywhere. If I had hit it hard enough to do any real damage, I'm sure there'd be a lump."

"Yeah," I agreed, "I'm sure you're fine." If she had actually hit her head, I would have insisted she go to the hospital, but, well, you know. Before my mom could think too much about things, I changed the subject. "Happy Christmas Eve," I said as if it was a question.

My mom smacked her palm to her forehead. "I completely forgot! Happy Christmas Eve Xoe. We better get cooking."

I sighed sarcastically. "If we must."

We always cooked Christmas Eve dinner in our pajamas, then showered and changed clothes before whoever we invited arrived. I raised my eyebrows at my mom's purple polo and jeans. "You're not in your pj's," I remarked.

She looked down as if just realizing her attire. "Oh!" she gasped. "I must have really been out of it last night."

I raised my eyebrow even farther and tapped my foot in mock impatience.

My mom rolled her eyes at me. "You start the coffee, I'll get changed."

I nodded and left my mom's room. I heard someone knocking as I began to descend the stairs, so I hurried the rest of the way, and even leapt over the last three stairs. I was feeling good-as-new. Let's hear it for being a demon!

I reached the door and looked out the peephole (I knew better than to just answer it anymore). Jason was waiting outside with a little cardboard carrying thing containing three coffees and a bag that I sincerely hoped contained Danishes.

I opened the door and took in our breakfast delivery man. He was dressed in a horrible Christmas sweater complete with snowmen and little laughing elves and a crisp new pair of jeans.

"I'll take the coffee," I began, "but I don't think I can allow that sweater in my house."

"Have a little Christmas spirit," he jested. "I come bearing Danishes."

"Well in that case," I swung the door open dramatically, "welcome to my humble abode."

He gave me a good-natured smirk. "You are too kind."

We both turned to see my mom coming down the stairs in full-blown footie pajamas done in blue and covered in snowflakes. It was a very sad day when I was the best dressed in green sweats and my old, ratty *Bauhaus* t-shirt.

"You better turn around now Jason," my mom called after she spotted us. "The day when Xoe and I cook is a very, scary, day."

"Don't scare him mom!" I shouted back. "He comes bearing sustenance!"

My mom came to stand before Jason. "In that case welcome, how are you at prepping turkeys?"

Jason sighed in resignation and handed me the coffee and Danishes. He slid one of the coffees out of the holder and disappeared into the kitchen. I smiled to myself, boys will do anything.

"Is Allison coming?" my mom asked as soon as we were alone.

Lucy's family required her to be home on Christmas Eve, but Allison always came to our dinners. "Yep," I answered. "Oh, and Chase."

My mom nodded. "What about Brian? I know you two aren't too close anymore."

Speaking of Brian, I still had that Christmas gift for him. He'd gone home after our reunion at Jason's apartment. I had to assume that he was even less inclined to talk to me now than ever. "I'll tell you in a minute," I answered, then turned to run back upstairs.

I went into my room to dig Brian's jersey out of my closet. I hadn't had a chance to wrap anything, but since he probably didn't want a gift from me to begin with, I doubted he'd care whether or not it was wrapped.

I trotted back downstairs with the jersey in hand, stopping to slip on some winter boots before heading out the front door. I looked down at the jersey as I trotted towards Brian's house, then skidded to a halt, almost running into Brian as he jogged towards me.

We stared at each other a moment, then I held out the jersey. He took the jersey with one hand and stuck the other one into his pocket. When his hand came back out something shiny came with it. He held out a dainty silver bracelet with a heart charm attached to the clasp. Upon closer examination I noticed that the charm had my name engraved on it.

I hesitantly took the bracelet from his outstretched hand. "Since when do you get me jewelry?" I asked with a smile.

Brian looked down at the ground as he answered. "Since everything changed."

My smile wilted around the edges. I wasn't sure where he was going with this. I waited in silence for him to elaborate.

"I'm going to try harder to be your friend Xoe," he said finally meeting my eyes. "I abandoned you because I couldn't handle the . . . changes in your life, when I should have been there to help you handle them."

A glimmer of hope surfaced in my mind. Too bad I had to squash it. "Being my friend puts you in danger Brian. You have to think carefully about this choice. I'll understand if you say we can't be friends. I just need closure one way or the other."

Brian's brow furrowed into angry lines. "We're friends Xoe. End of story. I may not be able to handle everything all at once, but we're both going to work on this friendship if it kills us."

"It very well may," I mumbled.

Brian sighed. "Shut up and invite me inside."

I raised an eyebrow at him. "Are you sure? You risk great peril."

Brian grinned. "I've eaten your cooking before Xoe."

I playfully punched Brian in the arm, then turned to walk back up my driveway. As we reached my door, I noticed a small burgundy box with an understated gold bow tied around it. Brian stooped to pick it up. He turned it over in his palm, then handed it to me with a shrug. "No name on it."

I took the offered box and walked to sit down on my front porch swing. "Go on inside," I told Brian. "Make sure my mom doesn't burn down the house.

Brian gave me a final considering look, then let himself into my house. I stared at the box for several minutes before finally untying the delicate gold bow. I removed the lid to reveal a somewhat gaudy ring and a folded piece of stationary. I slipped the ring onto my index finger then unfolded the note. It read simply:

This ring is a family heirloom. Its origins are unknown, as are its magical properties. Have a merry Christmas, and give Libby my best.

-A

Well, the A had to stand for Alexondre. I placed the note back inside the box and examined the ring more closely. It was composed of a brownish red gemstone the size of my thumbnail set in delicate, spiraling silver designs that twisted to form the band of the ring. As I watched, a flare of light emanated from the center of the stone. I blinked my eyes in astonishment then looked at the stone again. As far as I could tell it was an ordinary stone once more. I'd have to ask my dad about it at our first official lesson. I gathered up the box and ribbon and headed into the warmth of my house.

Over the next few hours I helped my mom bake and mash and baste while Jason and Brian tried to be cordial over a game of chess. By the time Lucy, Max, and Allison showed up, my mom and I had both showered, and the boys had managed to set the table with mismatched plates and silverware.

I was beginning to think that Chase would be a no-show when the doorbell rang. I answered the door to find him standing in a deep red button up shirt and charcoal gray slacks.

I raised an eyebrow at him. "You know this is a casual event, right?"

Chase shrugged. "I've never been to a Christmas dinner before."

My jaw dropped. "*Never?*"

Chase shrugged again, seeming embarrassed. I tried to usher him inside as a change of subject, but instead he grabbed my hand and led me out onto the porch, closing the door behind us.

"I wasn't sure if I should get you anything . . . " he began as he fished around in his pocket to pull out a small gray box. He handed me the box, then watch expectantly for me to open it.

I cracked the lid to find a charm in the shape of a curling serpent, with tiny green gems for eyes. "Gee," I began, "I go my whole life without anyone buying me jewelry, then I get it all in one day."

"If you don't like it . . . " Chase began.

"Oh no," I cut him off. "It's perfect." I held up my wrist with Brian's bracelet, and twisted the loop of the charm onto the clasp with the heart on it.

Chase smiled and met my eyes and the moment suddenly became way too intimate. I blushed and grabbed his arm to usher him inside. As we came through the front door we ran into Jason, apparently coming to check on me. Chase relinquished my arm and the three of us walked awkwardly to join everyone else at the table.

The dinner was interesting, to say the least. The mashed potatoes closely resembled soup, and the candied yams probably weren't supposed to be tinged with gray, but at least the turkey came out perfectly. That was probably because Jason cooked it, but no one needed to know that little fact.

We all served ourselves, and much to my chagrin everyone avoided the yams. Out of spite I stood and grabbed the bowl, the proceeded to pile a heaping spoonful onto everyone's plates. Lucy was the first trooper to place a dainty bite into her mouth. We all waited while she started to chew, then laughed as she ran into the kitchen to spit the bite back out.

All seemed well again in the Meyer's household and we finished dinner and watched old clay-mation Christmas movies together. By midnight everyone had passed out except for Jason and me. Allison and Max fell asleep holding hands. Who saw that one coming?

Jason and I crept upstairs to my room where we snuggled up with my comforter wrapped around us. I reached over the end of the bed and pulled out the books I got Jason. I hadn't got around to wrapping them, but figured Jason wouldn't really mind. He accepted the books with what I hoped wasn't fake enthusiasm.

He stood up and gave me a quick kiss on the forehead. "I'll be right back, your gift is in my car."

With a blur of motion he hopped out of my window. I was left to wait alone on my bed and reflect. When the year had started I led a normal life. Now I had a boyfriend, a dad, a werewolf pack, and Chase. I wasn't too keen on investigating what I meant to Chase. Ignore it and it would go away? Doubtful, very doubtful. The more disturbing question was whether I really wanted him to go away.

Jason interrupted my thoughts as he popped back into my room through my window. He handed me a rectangular box wrapped in bright, reindeer covered wrapping paper with a big red bow on it.

"Tell me it's not jewelry," I said sarcastically.

Not understanding my humor Jason cocked his head in confusion.

I shook my head. "Nevermind."

I tore open the wrapping paper and let it fall to the floor to reveal a box with a pretty laptop computer on it. I shook the box by my ear. "Is it . . . shoes?"

"No," Jason laughed.

"A puppy?" I questioned.

Jason grinned and took the box from me so he could open it and pull the computer out of it. He set it on my lap for me to examine. I looked up at my ancient hand-me-down desktop computer, then back at my laptop. I smiled. "I knew I should have bought you something better than books."

Chapter Seventeen

The next day was the least eventful day I'd had all week. Able had shown up personally to apologize for not reaching Shelby in time to help. He wished me a merry Christmas, then left with a knowing smile and a 'see you soon.'

School would start up again soon, along with my how to be a demon lessons. Even more daunting was the looming coalition meeting. I still didn't know how I was going to convince my mom to let me go.

All of those worries were for another day. Just for Christmas, I ignored all of my worries. I went sledding and watched more Christmas movies with my mom and Jason. I was somehow happy with my new strange life. And that was worrisome enough.

CPSIA information can be obtained
at www.ICGtesting.com
Printed in the USA
LVOW03s1915310717
543282LV00001B/19/P